D1241085

"C" IS FOR CUPCAKE

Published by Harcourt, Brace & World

PENNY AND PETER. 1946
BETSY AND THE BOYS. 1945
HERE'S A PENNY. 1944
BACK TO SCHOOL WITH BETSY. 1943
PRIMROSE DAY. 1942
BETSY AND BILLY. 1941
TWO AND TWO ARE FOUR. 1940
"B" IS FOR BETSY. 1939

By the Same Author

Published by William Morrow & Company

AWAY WENT THE BALLOONS. 1973
A CHRISTMAS FANTASY. 1972
EDDIE'S HAPPENINGS. 1971
MERRY CHRISTMAS FROM BETSY. 1970
TAFFY AND MELISSA MOLASSES. 1969
EVER-READY EDDIE. 1968
BETSY AND MR. KILPATRICK. 1967
EDDIE THE DOG HOLDER. 1966
ROBERT ROWS THE RIVER. 1965
EDDIE'S GREEN THUMB. 1964
HERE COMES THE BUS! 1963
SNOWBOUND WITH BETSY. 1962
ANNIE PAT AND EDDIE. 1960
EDDIE AND LOUELLA. 1959
BETSY'S WINTERHOUSE. 1958
EDDIE MAKES MUSIC. 1957
BETSY'S BUSY SUMMER. 1956
EDDIE AND HIS BIG DEALS. 1955
BETSY AND THE CIRCUS. 1954
EDDIE'S PAY DIRT. 1953
THE MIXED-UP TWINS. 1952
EDDIE AND GARDENIA. 1951
BETSY'S LITTLE STAR. 1950
EDDIE AND THE FIRE ENGINE. 1949
PENNY GOES TO CAMP. 1948
LITTLE EDDIE. 1947

"C" IS FOR CUPCAKE

written and illustrated by

Carolyn Haywood

William Morrow and Company

New York 1974

Printed in the United States of America.
1 2 3 4 5 78 77 76 75 74

Library of Congress Cataloging in Publication Data

Haywood, Carolyn (date)
"C" is for cupcake.

SUMMARY: Adventures of Christie, her rabbit, Cupcake, and other members of her first grade class.
[1. School stories] I. Title.
PZ7.H31496Cai [Fic] 73-9282
ISBN 0-688-20098-2
ISBN 0-688-30098-7 (lib. bdg.)

Dedicated with Love
to My Two Little Cousins,
Laura Lew
and
Pamela Lew.

ACKNOWLEDGMENT

The author wishes to express her appreciation to the following teachers and librarians who have been helpful in talking to her freely about school activities and in making valuable suggestions:

Ann Githins,
principal of Cynwyd Elementary School

Gertrude Emmerling,
whose first grade I visited many times

Selma Lucca,
who told me about the arrival of the rabbit

Kendall Kanasky,
librarian at Blue Bell School

Linda Fine,
of the Philadelphia Free Library

CONTENTS

Chapter 1

A RABBIT NAMED CUPCAKE

CHRISTIE was in the first grade. She hadn't been in the first grade very long. She had been there just long enough to learn to print her name on the line at the top of the green paper. Christie thought the green paper was very pretty. It was pale green with dark green lines.

Christie took a long time to print her name, because her full name was Christine. Her friend Mark could print his quickly—*Mark*. So could Sara—*Sara!*

Sometimes they watched Christie printing her name. Sara would say, "Hurry up!"

Mark would say, "Christie's a slowpoke!"

"It's hard," Christie would reply, "when your name is Christine."

The first-grade room was a happy place. It was a big room with many windows on two sides. On sunny days the room was filled with sunshine. On dark days the lights in the ceiling made the room cheerful. One wall was covered with a large blackboard. The other side had big closets. Christie thought they were the funniest closets she had ever seen. When she opened one of the closet doors, all of the doors flew open. The closets had shelves that held books and all kinds of paper and the many things that Christie's teacher, Mrs. Wilkins, needed in the class.

The room was furnished with large tables and many little chairs. There was a big chair and a large desk for Mrs. Wilkins. Christie thought the nicest thing in the room was a big sofa. It had very short legs, so a child could climb into it easily. There were soft pillows on the sofa. It was a cozy place to curl up with a picture book.

There was a television and a popcorn popper. Christie wasn't surprised to find a television in her classroom, but she had not expected a popcorn popper. She hoped they would pop a lot of corn, for she loved popcorn.

Christie enjoyed school, but she wished she could have Cupcake with her. Cupcake was her white rabbit. Her fur was thick, and her ears were long. She had a pink nose, which twitched and wiggled. When she was a tiny bunny, she had been an Easter present for Christie. Now she filled Christie's arms. Christie loved her very much.

Christie's father had made Cupcake's cage. It

had a floor of wood and wooden uprights at each corner. The sides of the cage were made of wire screening and the top of chicken wire. It had large holes in it. "You can drop the rabbit's food through these holes," her father said to Christie. Her father built the cage out-of-doors. He had meant to build a small cage, but when it was finished it was almost as big as a bathtub.

One day Mrs. Wilkins said, "Children, next Monday is Cupcake Day!"

Christie was surprised. Her big brown eyes seemed bigger than ever as she called out to her teacher, "Cupcake Day?"

"That's right!" Mrs. Wilkins replied. "Cupcake Day! We have one every month, but this is the first one for you children, so I shall give you each a note to take home to your mothers. I'll pin the notes on your coats so you won't lose them."

"I didn't wear a coat," said Mark. "I wore a sweater."

"Then I'll pin the note on your sweater," said Mrs. Wilkins.

When the children from Mrs. Wilkins's first grade climbed into the school bus, a piece of white paper was pinned on each child.

Christie sat down beside Mark. "Just think, Mark," she said, "Cupcake is going to have a whole day. 'Magin that! Just like George Washington! A whole day for herself!"

"I like cupcakes," said Mark. "I like chocolate cupcakes. They're good!"

"Silly!" said Christie. "Cupcake is a rabbit."

Mark laughed and called out to all the children on the bus, "Christie says cupcakes are rabbits!" All the children laughed.

Just as Christie jumped off the bus, she met her mother. She was carrying a big bag of groceries. "Oh, Mommy!" she cried. "You'll never guess! Next Monday is Cupcake Day. Cupcake is going to have a whole day just for her! I can take her to school."

"Whatever do you mean?" her mother asked.

"It's all on this piece of paper," said Christie. "See? It's pinned to my coat."

"I'll read it when we get home," said her mother.

As they walked together Christie talked about Cupcake. "It will be fun to have Cupcake in school with me. Will we take her cage or will she just run free? Will I carry her in my arms? I guess I'll have to carry her."

Christie didn't wait to hear what her mother answered. The questions just tumbled off her lips, one after another. Finally she said, "What do you think, Mommy?"

"I don't know," her mother replied, as she opened the front door. "I'll read the note as soon as I can put down this big bag of groceries."

Christie followed her mother into the kitchen. "See!" said Christie. "Here's the paper pinned to my coat."

Christie's mother leaned over and unfastened the note. She opened it and read it out loud. "Cupcake Day is held at our school once every month. Next Monday is Cupcake Day, and we

hope the mothers will make some cupcakes. They are sold to the children at lunchtime to raise funds to buy books for the school library."

Christie's mother looked down at Christie's eager face and said, "Why, Christie, the note isn't about your rabbit. Cupcake Day is the day they sell cupcakes at school."

Christie looked as though she was about to cry. "Do you mean the kind of cupcakes we eat?" she asked.

"That's right," her mother replied. "The mothers make the cupcakes for the school."

Christie's face looked a bit brighter now. "And do the children eat them?" she asked.

Her mother laughed. "I imagine so, if the children buy them," she said.

"Are you going to make some cupcakes?" Christie asked next.

"Yes, I'll make some," her mother answered, as she unpacked the bag of groceries, "and if you are very careful, you can carry the cupcakes into the school."

"Carrying cupcakes isn't as much fun as carrying Cupcake," said Christie, pouting again. "I want to carry Cupcake to school. That's what I want." Christie ran off to feed her rabbit.

The following day Christie said to Mrs. Wilkins, "Please, Mrs. Wilkins, can I bring Cupcake to school?"

"Yes, on Monday, Christie," her teacher replied. "Monday is Cupcake Day."

"You mean on Monday I can bring Cupcake?" Christie asked again.

"Well, not just one cupcake, Christie," said Mrs. Wilkins. "Several cupcakes."

"But my Cupcake is only one," said Christie. "What I want to know is whether I can bring Cupcake on Cupcake Day when I bring the cupcakes."

Mrs. Wilkins sat down at her desk. She put her arm around Christie. "Now, Christie," she said, "tell me very slowly. How many cupcakes are you talking about?"

Christie took a deep breath. Then she said, "There's just one Cupcake, but my mommy says I can bring twelve cupcakes. What I want to know is, when I bring the twelve cupcakes, can I bring Cupcake?"

Mrs. Wilkins thought about this question. She looked puzzled. There were wrinkles across her forehead, but she said, "Yes, I guess so. One more cupcake won't make any difference."

When Christie reached home that afternoon, she said to her mother, "Mrs. Wilkins says I can bring Cupcake to school on Monday. Isn't that wonderful?"

"Are you sure?" her mother asked.

"Yes, I'm sure!" said Christie. "She said so."

"I suppose she wants Cupcake's cage, too?" her mother asked.

"I guess so," Christie replied. "She has to sleep in her cage."

"Very well," said her mother, "then you won't be able to go to school on the bus on Monday.

I'll have to take you and Cupcake and the cage and the cupcakes to school in the station wagon."

On Monday morning Christie said to her mother, "I want to carry Cupcake."

"You can't carry Cupcake and the box of cupcakes," said her mother. "You know how jumpy rabbits are!"

"Well, I guess she'll have to go to school in her cage," said Christie.

"No," said her mother, "she'll be frightened when I lift the cage in and out of the car. We had better put her in a cardboard box, so she won't be able to see what we are doing."

Christie's mother found a cardboard box in the cellar. She made holes in the lid with a knife.

Christie watched her mother. "What are the holes for?" she asked.

"So Cupcake can breathe," her mother replied.

"Oh, yes!" said Christie. "She has to breathe."

The cupcakes that her mother had baked were packed in a square box and tied with a string.

It wasn't easy for Christie's mother to get the cage into the station wagon, but after a good many grunts and "Oh, dears!" and with Christie's help she finally got the cage into the back of the station wagon. The box of cupcakes was on the seat of the car between Christie and her mother, and the box containing Cupcake was on Christie's lap.

"Now," said her mother, as she started the car, "carry the cupcakes carefully when we get to school. I don't want them to get broken in the box."

"I'll be careful," said Christie.

When they reached the school, they saw many boys and girls carrying boxes. "I bet there are a lot of cupcakes," said Christie. "All kinds of cupcakes. I can hardly wait to eat one of those cupcakes!"

"Think what you're doing," said her mother. "Take the box with the rabbit first. Then come back for the cupcakes. I'll bring the cage."

"All right!" Christie replied, as she stepped out of the car with the box that contained her rabbit. "I'll be right back."

When Christie reached her classroom, she placed Cupcake's box on Mrs. Wilkins's desk.

"Are these the cupcakes, Christie?" Mrs. Wilkins asked.

"This is Cupcake," said Christie. "Just put your hand on the lid and hold it down, so Cupcake doesn't jump out. 'Cause I have to go back to get the cupcakes."

"Jump out!" exclaimed Mrs. Wilkins. "What kind of a cupcake is it?"

"It's Cupcake, my rabbit, that you said I could bring. She won't jump out if you hold the lid down. It won't hurt her. You see she can breathe through these holes my mommy cut in the top. My mommy's bringing Cupcake's cage."

Mrs. Wilkins was so surprised that she couldn't speak. She just stood by her desk holding down the lid of the box.

Christie ran out of the room. Soon she was back with the box of cupcakes. "Oh, Christie!" said Mrs. Wilkins. "You have to take the cupcakes to the school office. And, please, tell your mother to hurry with the cage. I can't stand here holding this lid down forever."

"I'll tell her," said Christie, "but don't let Cupcake jump out." Christie disappeared with her box of cupcakes.

She was a long time coming back. When she

finally appeared, she said, "My mommy can't get the cage through the front door. The door's too little. Mommy says have you got a hammer so she can take the cage apart."

"It's a great big door!" exclaimed Mrs. Wilkins. "If the cage is too big to come through the front door, it is too big to come into this room, so there is no use giving your mother a hammer. What *have* you brought to school?" said Mrs. Wilkins. She was so excited that she forgot to keep her hand on the lid of the box. The lid flew up and out jumped Cupcake.

All the children yelled. "Oh, look at the rabbit!"

Christie ran after Cupcake and caught her. She held her in her arms and looked up at her teacher. "What shall we do?" she asked.

Mrs. Wilkins thought for a few minutes. Then she said, "There is a table in the yard behind the building. Tell your mother to put the cage on the table until we can decide what to do."

"What shall I do with Cupcake?" Christie asked.

"Put her in her cage," Mrs. Wilkins answered.

Christie's lip began to tremble. "Don't you like Cupcake?" she said, looking up at her teacher.

Mrs. Wilkins smoothed Cupcake's snowy white fur. "Of course, I like Cupcake," she said, "but she is a surprise. Just take her out and put her in her cage until I have time to think what to do with a rabbit named Cupcake on Cupcake Day."

Christie carried her rabbit back to her mother. She found her surrounded with children. They were all trying to help her get the cage through the front door of the school.

"Teacher says no hammer. She says put the cage on the table back of the school," said Christie.

"Oh," said her mother, "I'm glad I don't have to get the cage through that door."

Then, surrounded by a whole crowd of boys and girls eager to help, Christie's mother carried the cage to the table and set it down. Christie put Cupcake inside and said, "Well, Cupcake almost got to school, didn't she?"

The children stood around the cage admiring Cupcake. "She's a nice rabbit," they said to each other.

"Her name is Cupcake," said Christie.

"I'll bet Mrs. Wilkins will let her inside someday," said Mark.

"I hope so," said Christie, as they walked to the front door of the school. "Anyway she's almost there!"

Chapter 2

"C" IS FOR CHOCOLATE

CHRISTIE'S RABBIT Cupcake was soon inside the school. Her father built another cage for Cupcake. Not only did it go through the front door of the school, it went through the door into Christie's first-grade room. It, too, was made of wood. The sides were covered with wire netting, and the top with chicken wire. The new cage was placed in the corner of the room near the door. Over the weekends Christie took Cupcake home with her.

The next month when Cupcake Day came around, Mark came back from lunch very unhappy. His under lip was poked way out. When he spoke to Mrs. Wilkins, it trembled.

"What is the matter, Mark?" she asked.

"It's Cupcake Day," he said, "and I didn't get a chocolate cupcake. We only have Cupcake Day once a month, and I didn't get a chocolate cupcake."

"There weren't any chocolate ones," said Christie.

"Yes, there were," said Mark. "I saw you eating one."

"It was just chocolate icing," said Christie.

"Well, I didn't even get one with chocolate icing," said Mark. He was close to tears. "I like chocolate everything. Chocolate cake, chocolate ice cream, chocolate sauce, chocolate candy, chocolate milk, chocolate soda, chocolate brownies, chocolate fudge. Chocolate everything!"

As the children listened they thought about all these chocolate goodies, and their mouths began to water.

"Pretty soon," said Mark, "I'm going to have a birthday party, and it's going to be a Chocolate Birthday Party."

When the children heard about Mark's party, they all hoped that they would be invited to it.

"Mark," said Mrs. Wilkins, "do you know how to spell *chocolate*?"

"No," Mark replied.

"Well, I'll write it on the board," said Mrs. Wilkins. Picking up her piece of chalk, she wrote, *Chocolate*.

"Oh, my! That's a big word!" said Mark. "I guess it's because it's so good."

"That's as long as my name," said Christie.

Mrs. Wilkins laughed. "How many other children like chocolate?" she asked.

Every hand in the room went up, and every child called out, "I love chocolate!"

A week later, on Thursday, Christie received a card asking her to come to Mark's birthday party on the following Saturday. She was very pleased. She said to her mother, "It's going to be a chocolate party. Everything chocolate. Mark said so. He just loves chocolate!"

"That should be a nice party," said her mother.

"What shall I take to Mark for a present?" Christie asked.

"I'm sure he would like something made of chocolate," her mother replied, laughing.

"Like what?" Christie asked.

"I saw some chocolate soldiers in the window of the candy store on Main Street," said her mother.

"Oh, a chocolate soldier would be wonderful," said Christie. "Can we go buy it now?"

"I think we had better get it tomorrow when I go to market. We want to be sure that it's nice and fresh."

"You won't go without me, will you?" said Christie. " 'Cause I like to go to buy birthday presents."

"I'll wait until you come home from school," her mother promised.

When Christie and her mother went into the candy store, they could smell chocolate. The woman behind the counter smiled at them and said, "Good afternoon! What can I do for you?"

"We want to buy one of those chocolate soldiers," Christie's mother replied.

"It's for a birthday present," said Christie.

"For a little boy who is very fond of chocolate," said her mother.

"The chocolate soldiers are fresh in today,"

said the saleswoman, as she stood one on the counter.

Christie looked at the soldier. She thought it was beautiful, but it didn't look like chocolate. The soldier's face was pink. His cap and coat were bright blue, and his trousers were red. The gun over his shoulder shone like silver.

"Where's the chocolate?" Christie asked.

"Oh, the chocolate is inside," said the woman behind the counter. "When you take all the colored paper off, it's a very nice chocolate soldier."

"Yes," said Christie's mother. "It's covered with colored foil."

"Oh!" said Christie. "The kind you use in the kitchen to wrap the food. Only this is colored."

"That's right," said the woman. "It keeps the chocolate from melting, but still you have to be careful. You mustn't put the soldier near any heat."

When the soldier was placed in a cardboard

box, the woman handed the box to Christie. "Carry it carefully," she said. "I'm sure the little boy will be pleased with his birthday present."

Christie's mother paid for the gift and as they went out of the shop, the woman called after them, "Don't forget to keep it in a cool place."

When Christie and her mother reached home, Christie's mother said, "I think the best place to keep the chocolate soldier is in the refrigerator."

"Oh, can't I look at it?" said Christie. "I won't hurt it."

"Well, do be careful with it," said her mother, "and when you have finished looking at it, put it on a shelf in the refrigerator."

"I will," said Christie.

Christie's mother went into the kitchen to make a pie for dinner.

Christie carried the box with the chocolate soldier up to her bedroom. She opened the lid and looked down at the shiny soldier. Christie could hardly believe that it was made of chocolate. She picked it up and looked it over carefully. How could she see if it really was a chocolate soldier? She turned it over, hoping to find a place where the shiny covering might be loose. If it was, perhaps she could unwrap it just a tiny bit.

Christie looked all over the back of the soldier. She saw that the covering wasn't loose, but she noticed that the blue jacket was folded over right down the middle of the soldier's back. If she lifted the paper carefully, she was sure that she could put it together again. With her little fingernail she set about unfolding the jacket. As she lifted the edge of the paper a little speck of chocolate appeared. She leaned over the soldier and opened his jacket a little more. Now she could smell chocolate. She lifted it to her nose and sniffed. It did smell good!

Christie had just succeeded in uncovering the chocolate, when she heard her mother calling to her. "Christie, Margie is here! She's come to look at the T.V. show with you."

"I'm coming!" Christie called back. "Right away!"

Christie stood the soldier on the flat metal shelf that covered the radiator and hurried downstairs.

"Hello, Margie!" she said.

"Our T.V. is broken," said Margie, "so I came over to watch with you."

"I'm glad!" said Christie, as she opened the door for Margie to go into the room where the T.V. stood.

Christie turned on the set and sat down on the floor beside her friend. Then she said, "My mother and I just came back from the store. We went to buy a birthday present."

"I bought mine yesterday," said Margie.

"Who did you buy a birthday present for?" Christie asked.

"My mother said not to tell, because I might

tell somebody who hadn't been invited," said Margie. "That would make the person who hadn't been invited feel bad."

"Oh," said Christie, "I guess so."

The two little girls were quiet now. They watched the T.V. show and laughed at the puppets. In an hour it was over, and Christie turned off the T.V. set. Then she said, "Margie, if you'll tell me what the birthday present is that you bought, I'll show you the one I bought."

"Well, all right!" said Margie. "I guess I can tell you what the present is. It's a game!"

"Oh!" said Christie. "Well, come up to my room and see the present I have for—for"—she hesitated—"for somebody."

"Is it for a boy or a girl?" Margie asked.

"You didn't tell me whether your present is for a boy or a girl," said Christie, as she led the way upstairs.

When they walked into Christie's room, Margie said, "Yum, yum. I smell chocolate."

Christie smelled it too. She ran to the shelf over the radiator. What she saw made her scream, "Oh! Oh!"

Margie came to her. "What's that?" she said, pointing to a small heap of shiny red, blue, silver, and pink foil mixed up with a lot of melted chocolate.

"It was a chocolate soldier," cried Christie, with tears rolling down her cheeks. "My mother told me to put it in the refrigerator, and I forgot."

"Oh, that's awful!" said Margie. "But where is the birthday present?"

Christie pointed to the melted soldier on the shelf and said, very sorrowfully, "That's it."

"Oh," said Margie, "it's a mess, isn't it?" Margie stuck her finger into the chocolate and licked her finger.

"Don't do that!" Christie cried. "You'll spoil it."

"It's spoiled already," said Margie. "You

can't do anything with it now. We might as well eat it." Margie dipped into the chocolate again. "It's awfully good," she said.

Christie just looked at what had been the chocolate soldier and continued to cry. "Oh, what will my mother say!" she sobbed.

At that moment Christie's mother walked into the room. Christie ran to her and threw her arms about her mother's legs. "Oh, Mommy!" she cried. "The chocolate soldier for Mark's birthday! It's melted!"

Christie's mother looked at the remains of the chocolate soldier. "I told you, Christie, to put it in the refrigerator."

"I know! I know!" Christie sobbed. "I forgot! Oh, what will I do?"

"Right now you will clean up the mess," said her mother.

"I guess it's time for me to go," said Margie, moving toward the door. "If I had all that nice chocolate, I'd eat it."

"Christie is not going to eat it," said her

mother. "She is going to clean it up and throw it all away."

"Oh, dear!" said Margie. "Can't she have a teeny-weeny bit?"

"Not a teeny-weeny bit," replied Christie's mother.

"Well," said Margie, "I'll see you at Mark's birthday party. But I didn't tell you whose birthday party I'm going to, did I?"

"I don't remember," Christie replied, with a sniffle, as Margie went out the door. "I guess you didn't, but now I know."

"Come," said Christie's mother, "we'll go down to the kitchen and get some things to clean this up. Get a paper bag to put it in, and I'll throw it away."

"It smells like nice chocolate," said Christie, still with a sniffle. "Can't I taste it?"

"No, you cannot taste it," said her mother. "You were a careless little girl."

"What about Mark's birthday present?" Christie asked, as she burst into tears once more. "I can't go to the party without a birthday present."

"We'll talk about that later," her mother replied.

That evening when Christie was in bed, her mother came to say good-night. "Mommy, what about Mark's birthday present?"

"I've been thinking about it," her mother answered. "If you have enough money in your bank to buy another chocolate soldier, you may buy one. I am not going to pay for it."

"I'll see if I have enough money," said Christie. Her mother kissed her good-night, and Christie began to wonder about the money in her bank. She couldn't get to sleep, so she turned on the light and got up. She opened the closet where she kept her bank. Then she shuffled around in a drawer, trying to find the key to the bank. In the quiet room she sounded like a little mouse.

Oh, what would she do if she couldn't find the key! Her money would be locked up forever,

she thought. There were all kinds of things in the drawer. Christie grew more and more worried, but finally she found it. The key was inside a doll's shoe. She opened the bank, and her money fell out on her bed.

Christie was sorry to see that most of the coins were pennies, but there were other ones too. She set to work counting them. She counted all the pennies first. After a long time she finished. There were sixty-four pennies. Then she looked at the smaller coins. They were ten cents each. She counted nine of them. A number of coins were still left over. They all looked like silver, but some were larger than others. She counted them. There were five big ones and eight smaller ones.

Christie looked at her money spread out on the bed, but she didn't know how much she had. She didn't know whether it was enough to buy another chocolate soldier for Mark, but she hoped it was. Christie gathered up all of her coins and put them in her bank. Then she got back into bed and put out the light. Soon she was sound asleep.

As soon as Christie woke up, she remembered her money. She heard her mother in the kitchen, so she hopped out of bed. She put on her bathrobe and bedroom slippers and padded down the stairs with her bank in her hands.

"Mommy!" she said, when she reached the kitchen. "Please count my money so I'll know whether I can buy another chocolate soldier." Christie poured the coins onto the kitchen table and watched while her mother counted them. "Is it enough? Is it enough?" Christie said over and over again, while her mother counted the money.

"It is enough!" said her mother, gathering up the coins. "You have three dollars and nineteen cents, so there will be a bit left over."

"Oh, goodie!" Christie cried. "We'll have to go to buy the chocolate soldier this morning, because the party is this afternoon."

"We'll go right after breakfast," said her mother.

"They'll be sure to have another one, won't they?" Christie asked.

"I hope so," her mother answered. "They had several yesterday."

As soon as breakfast was over, Christie and her mother went back to the candy store. When they went in, the woman behind the counter said, "So you're back again! What can I do for you this morning?"

"We want another chocolate soldier," said

Christie's mother. "The other one came to a sorry end."

"Oh, that's too bad," said the woman, "because I haven't any more chocolate soldiers."

Tears came into Christie's eyes. "No more chocolate soldiers!" she murmured.

"No," said the saleswoman, "I only have one piece of chocolate left. It's a rabbit!" As she spoke she placed a chocolate rabbit on the counter.

Christie looked at the rabbit. "It isn't wrapped up the way the soldier was," she said.

"No," said the saleswoman. "They never wrap the rabbits. I guess they like them just as they are. Brown rabbits."

Christie did not look happy. "I think Mark would have liked the soldier," she said.

"But there isn't any soldier," said her mother, "so Mark will have to have a rabbit. At least it's chocolate." Then to cheer Christie, she added, "Don't you think it looks a bit like Cupcake?"

Christie smiled for the first time. "Yes, only Cupcake is white," she said.

Christie was very careful with the chocolate rabbit. When she got home, she put it in the refrigerator. Every once in a while, she peeked in to see if it was all right. She could hardly wait to go to the party! If anything happened to this rabbit, there was no way for her to get another one.

At last the time came to go. Christie ran with the precious box in her hand. When she finally handed it to Mark, she sighed and sat down.

Mark said, "Thank you," and opened the box. When he saw the chocolate rabbit, he laughed. "Oh, it's a rabbit. It's a chocolate Cupcake!"

When the rest of the children saw the chocolate rabbit, they all shouted, "Mark's got a chocolate Cupcake!"

Christie was glad now that the candy store had been out of chocolate soldiers and that she had brought Mark a chocolate Cupcake.

Chapter 3

AND FOR CORNFLAKES

THE DAY Cupcake was brought into the first-grade classroom, she seemed nervous and twitchy. Mrs. Wilkins told the children not to pet her until she got used to her new home.

When Mrs. Wilkins was busy, writing some new words on the blackboard, Chuckie Carpenter took Cupcake out of her cage. He hadn't learned how to lift a rabbit properly by the loose skin on the back of its neck. Instead he picked her up by her ears, which hurt her, and Cupcake struggled in Chuckie's hands. Still, how she happened to kick Chuckie in the chin, no one knew. Chuckie yelled and dropped Cupcake. "She kicked me!" he cried. "That old rabbit kicked me."

Christie picked up her rabbit and comforted her. Then she put Cupcake back in her cage.

Mrs. Wilkins called Chuckie to her and said, "I told you not to touch the rabbit until she felt at home here."

"I know," said Chuckie, "but look what she did to me, Mrs. Wilkins. She kicked me right on the chin."

Mrs. Wilkins looked at Chuckie's chin. "You're making a fuss over nothing, Chuckie. Now don't touch the rabbit again."

"I won't!" said Chuckie, rubbing his chin.

"I won't ever touch her! Never!" From then on Chuckie disliked Cupcake, and he let everyone know how he felt.

Soon Cupcake seemed very happy in the first grade. The children fed her carrots and lettuce. They were always bringing food for Cupcake, and Mrs. Wilkins had to watch that she didn't eat too much.

Cupcake's favorite food was cornflakes. She ate her cornflakes out of the children's hands. They liked to feel her wiggly nose and her whiskers against their skin. They would laugh and say, "She tickles!"

Cupcake was taken out many times during the day, because the children liked to pet her. Only Chuckie kept away from her. He never petted her and never fed cornflakes to her. But he ate her cornflakes whenever he had a chance. Chuckie was a chubby little boy, and it was nibble, nibble, nibble, crunch, crunch, crunch all the time with him.

"You're eating Cupcake's cornflakes!" Christie would say. "I hear you."

"I like cornflakes!" Chuckie would reply.

"Well, my mother doesn't buy cornflakes for you," Christie would say. "She buys them for Cupcake."

One day Chuckie carried cornflakes in both his hands to the lunchroom at lunchtime. All the way down the hall he dropped cornflakes. When he reached the lunchroom, he put the ones that were left into a cup and poured milk over them.

When Christie saw what Chuckie was doing, she said, "Are you eating Cupcake's cornflakes again?"

"Yep!" Chuckie replied. "I'm just as good as that old rabbit." Crunch! Crunch! Crunch!

"Now I'll have to bring more for Cupcake," said Christie.

"I'll eat them too," said Chuckie. Crunch! Crunch! Crunch!

"You'll get sick," said Christie.

"Cornflakes don't make you sick," said Chuckie. "They're good for you. I'll bet I could eat a whole box and it wouldn't make me sick."

"You couldn't eat a whole box of cornflakes," said Bruce, who was sitting near Chuckie. "Your tummy would burst."

"I could too," said Chuckie, as he ate the last spoonful.

"That's why he's so fat," said Mark.

A few days later Christie saw Chuckie standing in front of Cupcake's cage. His back was to Christie. Christie wondered what Chuckie was doing. A strange sound was coming from the cage. Christie went over to find out what it was. When she reached Chuckie's side, she saw that he was scraping the wire screening of the cage with the lid of a tin can.

"Chuckie," said Christie, "what are you doing to Cupcake?"

"I'm not doing anything to your old rabbit," Chuckie replied.

"You're scratching her cage, and you'll make a hole in it," said Christie.

"I will not," said Chuckie. "I just like to hear the noise."

Mrs. Wilkins, who was helping some of the children to read, looked over at Chuckie and said, "Stop what you're doing on the rabbit's cage. The sound is very annoying."

Another day Christie again found Chuckie scraping the cage. "Stop that, Chuckie!" she said. "Stop it!"

"You and your old rabbit," said Chuckie, as he walked away from the cage.

About a week later Christie went to see Cupcake, as she always did, before school began. Cupcake was nibbling a lettuce leaf, but as Christie looked into the cage she noticed a little hole in the wire screening. "Oh, Mrs. Wilkins!" Christie called to her teacher. "There's a hole in Cupcake's cage."

Mrs. Wilkins came to Christie's side and looked at the cage. She saw the little hole.

Just then Chuckie came into the room. "Chuckie," she said, "did you make this hole in the rabbit's cage?"

"I never did," Chuckie replied.

"He did!" said Christie. "I heard him scraping yesterday."

"I only scraped it a little bit," said Chuckie.

"I told you not to scrape it at all," said Mrs. Wilkins. "There is a hole there now."

"Oh, dear!" Christie sighed. "Now Cupcake may get out of the cage and get lost."

"That old rabbit!" said Chuckie. "We'd see her if she got out. Anybody could see a white rabbit running around the room."

"But she might get out at night when nobody is here," said Christie.

"Don't worry," said Mrs. Wilkins. "It was very wrong for Chuckie to make the hole, but I'm sure it is too little for Cupcake to squeeze through."

* * *

The following morning, when Christie looked into Cupcake's cage, the cage was empty. Christie turned to the children in the room and said, "Who has Cupcake?" There was no answer.

Christie was frightened. She ran to Mrs. Wilkins and asked, "Where's Cupcake?"

"I don't know," Mrs. Wilkins replied. "Somebody must have her." But when she asked the children, they all said that they had not seen Cupcake.

Christie began to cry. "She's gone!" she sobbed. "She got through that hole. I knew she would. I knew it."

"I can't see how she could have pushed herself through that little hole," said Mrs. Wilkins. "I'm sure she was in the cage this morning when I came in. I haven't left the room."

"Excuse me, Mrs. Wilkins, but you weren't here when I came in. Only Chuckie was here," said Margie.

"You're right, Margie," said Mrs. Wilkins. "I

did leave the room. I went to the office to speak to Mr. Evans." Mr. Evans was the principal of the school. "Chuckie, was the door open when you came in?"

"I didn't look," replied Chuckie.

"You must remember whether you opened the door to come into the room," said Mrs. Wilkins. "If the door was open, Cupcake may be in some other part of the school."

"I don't remember," said Chuckie.

As Christie walked across the room, she stepped on cornflakes. Crunch! Crunch! "Somebody's been in the cornflakes," she said.

"Chuckie, I'll bet!" said Bruce.

Christie looked back at the stool where the box of cornflakes always stood. The box was gone. "Mrs. Wilkins," she called out, "the box of cornflakes is gone!"

"I guess Cupcake took it with her," Chuckie called out. All the children laughed, all but Christie. She was still crying.

"Now, Christie!" said Mrs. Wilkins. "Crying

will not bring Cupcake back. Wash your face and dry your tears. Then go to each room on this floor, and see if anyone has seen Cupcake."

Christie went into the washroom and put cold water on her face. When she had dried her face, her eyes and nose didn't look so red. She started out to see if Cupcake was in one of the other rooms. In each room she asked, "Has anyone seen a white rabbit?"

When Christie asked in the second-grade room, a girl said, "I saw a boy with a white rabbit this morning. He was running with it."

"Where was he running?" Christie asked.

"I don't know," the girl replied. "He was just running with it."

When Christie returned to her room, she looked very sad. "I didn't find her," she said. "A girl in the second grade said she saw a boy running with a white rabbit."

"Running where?" Mrs. Wilkins asked.

"She didn't know," Christie answered.

"This is very strange," said Mrs. Wilkins.

"Maybe somebody hid her," said Margie.

"Somebody who wanted to get rid of her," said Bruce.

"Yes," said Christie, "somebody who doesn't like her." She looked right at Chuckie.

"Yes, somebody who doesn't like her," said Mark, "but likes to eat her cornflakes."

Just then one of the school bus drivers opened the door. "Has anybody lost a white rabbit?" he asked, holding up Cupcake.

Christie cried, "Oh!" and ran to the bus driver. She stretched out her arms and shouted, "She's mine! It's Cupcake!" The bus driver put Cupcake into Christie's arms. She held Cupcake close and patted her. "Poor Cupcake!" she murmured. "Did you get lost?" Christie was so glad to have Cupcake back that she felt tears come into her eyes again, but this time the tears were for joy.

"Where did you find her?" Mrs. Wilkins asked the bus driver.

"Well, it's like this," he said. "After I brought my busload of children here, I went into the lunchroom to have a cup of coffee. When I came back, there was this rabbit sitting in my bus. I don't see how she got there. A little thing like that couldn't have jumped up all those steps. Somebody must have put her in the bus."

"Thank you very much for bringing her back to us," said Mrs. Wilkins.

"You're quite welcome," the bus driver re-

plied. "They told me down the hall that a little girl had been looking for a rabbit."

"You didn't find the box of cornflakes, did you?" Christie asked.

"Cornflakes!" exclaimed the man. "No, I didn't see any box of cornflakes."

The bus driver went out of the room and closed the door.

"Now!" said Mrs. Wilkins to the children. "I want to know who put Cupcake in the school bus."

The children sat quietly at the tables. They could hear the clock ticking. No one said a word.

Then Christie spoke up and said, "It was a boy. That's what the girl in the second grade said. It was a boy!"

"I want every boy to look at me," said Mrs. Wilkins.

Every boy in the room looked up at Mrs. Wilkins, but Chuckie hung his head.

"Chuckie," said Mrs. Wilkins, "did you put

Cupcake in the bus?" Chuckie's head hung lower. "Answer me, Chuckie. Why did you do it?"

"Well, I found her out in the hall," said Chuckie, "and I thought it would be fun to hide her. I knew the bus driver would bring her back. Anyway I don't like that rabbit. She kicked me in the chin."

"You should forgive Cupcake," said Mrs. Wilkins. "Perhaps you hurt her."

"I don't like her," said Chuckie.

Christie spoke up. "He likes Cupcake's cornflakes, he does."

"Yes!" said Mrs. Wilkins. "Where is the box of cornflakes, Chuckie?"

"They're inside me," Chuckie muttered.

The children gasped! "It was a whole box!" Christie cried out.

"Chuckie!" Mrs. Wilkins exclaimed. "You couldn't have eaten a whole box of cornflakes. Where are the cornflakes?"

Again Chuckie said, "Inside me."

"Chuckie will burst, won't he?" said Bruce. "Won't he burst?"

"Chuckie, come here to me," said Mrs. Wilkins.

Chuckie walked over to Mrs. Wilkins. She looked down at him. His striped shirt seemed very tight. Suddenly two buttons flew off. The buttons were followed by a shower of cornflakes, for Chuckie had poured the box of cornflakes inside his shirt.

"Chuckie," said Mrs. Wilkins, "why did you put the cornflakes inside your shirt?"

" 'Cause I like cornflakes," Chuckie replied.

"He busted, didn't he?" Bruce cried out. And just then Cupcake burst through the hole in her cage and began nibbling the cornflakes.

Christie ran and picked her up. "See!" she said. "Cupcake did get through that little hole. Now I'll have to take her home until her cage is mended."

At the end of the day, as Christie was carrying Cupcake out of the room to take her home for the weekend, Chuckie said, "Hey, Christie! Don't forget to bring another box of cornflakes on Monday."

"I'm not going to bring any more cornflakes," said Christie. "Cupcake will have to eat oatmeal."

"Not cooked?" Chuckie asked.

"Not cooked," Christie replied.

"I don't like oatmeal unless it's cooked," said Chuckie.

"Well, that's good!" Christie answered, as she walked away with her rabbit.

The hole in Cupcake's cage was patched with a piece of wire netting, and Christie felt comforted knowing that her rabbit was safe. She brought a box of oatmeal to school instead of cornflakes, and Cupcake seemed just as happy to eat oatmeal out of the children's hands.

Chapter 4

AND FOR CAKE AND CROWN

WHENEVER anyone in Christie's first grade had a birthday, they celebrated with a make-believe birthday cake with candles. It was made of a round cardboard box covered with something that looked like pink icing. When it was not being used, it was kept on a plate under a glass cover. Because it never got dusty, it always looked like a freshly baked birthday cake. Although it couldn't be eaten, each child on his birthday enjoyed blowing out the pink candles. Then all the children ate what they called birthday cookies.

The make-believe birthday cake was often borrowed by other classes in the school. Sometimes they forgot to return it. Then when a first-grade child was having a birthday, the whole school had to be searched in order to find the birthday cake.

One day, when Mrs. Wilkins needed a long time to find the birthday cake, she said, "If we just had an oven, we could bake our birthday cakes."

The following Monday morning Bruce rushed into the room and said to Mrs. Wilkins, "I've brought a present! Daddy is bringing it in."

"Oh, Bruce!" Mrs. Wilkins exclaimed. "It isn't another cage with an animal, is it?"

"No!" Bruce answered. "It's just what you wanted. It's an oven! We got a new one at our house, and my father said I could bring the old one to school. I told my father you would like it."

"An oven!" exclaimed Mrs. Wilkins. "How big is the oven?"

"Oh, it's big enough to roast a turkey," Bruce replied. "My mother roasted turkeys in it."

Just then Bruce's father appeared at the door with the oven. The big electric cord hung down like a tail. Mrs. Wilkins was glad to see that the oven was not as big as the rabbit's cage. "See!" said Bruce. "It's big enough to roast a turkey."

"Why, Mr. Cramer!" said Mrs. Wilkins. "How nice of you to bring us an oven! I'll clear off a table so that you can put it down."

As Mrs. Wilkins cleared a table, the children watched and asked questions. "Are we going to cook a turkey, Mrs. Wilkins? When can we cook? We don't have any pots and pans. Will we get pots and pans?"

At last Bruce's father placed the oven on the table. "Well, have fun!" he said to Mrs. Wilkins.

"Thank you very much," said Mrs. Wilkins. "This is a very fine present. Now we shall all learn to cook."

As Bruce's father left the room, he laughed and said, "I hope I'll be invited to eat some of the cooking."

"Indeed, we won't forget you," Mrs. Wilkins replied.

When the door closed, Chuckie said, "See if it works. Maybe it doesn't work."

"Course it works!" said Bruce. "My father wouldn't give us an oven that didn't work."

Bruce plugged the cord into the nearest outlet. The children gathered around the oven. When they saw two rods inside turn from black to bright orange, they shouted, "It works!"

Christie clapped her hands and said, "Oh, Mrs. Wilkins! Now we can make birthday cakes! We'll have real birthday cakes!"

"Oh, yes!" the children cried. "Real birthday cakes! How soon can we make a birthday cake?"

"My birthday is next Friday," said Debbie.

"Oh, Debbie!" said Christie. "You'll have the first real birthday cake, and we'll all bake it for you. What kind do you want?"

Debbie stood with her finger in her mouth. She was thinking. At last she said, "I want one with pink icing and pink candles."

Christie turned to Mrs. Wilkins and said, "Can Debbie have a cake with pink icing and pink candles?"

"Indeed, she can," Mrs. Wilkins replied. "We'll make it for her on Thursday afternoon."

"Why not Friday morning?" Mark asked. "Why do we have to make it on Thursday afternoon?"

"Because we go to assembly on Friday morning," Mrs. Wilkins replied. "The third grade is going to give a play. There wouldn't be time to bake a cake on Friday morning."

"I can't wait to help bake that cake," said Margie.

"I can't wait to eat a piece of it," said Chuckie.

Mrs. Wilkins gathered the children around her. "Come," she said, "come, sit on the floor. I'm going to read you a story."

The children settled down on the floor, but before Mrs. Wilkins had time to open the book, Margie raised her hand. "I have something to share!" she said.

"What do you want to tell us?" Mrs. Wilkins asked.

Margie stood up and faced the other children. "It's about birthdays. At our house we wear a crown on our birthdays. Whoever has a birthday wears a crown all day long."

"Oh!" exclaimed Christie. "I think we should have a crown here in school. If we had a crown, Debbie could wear it on her birthday."

"Yes, we should have a crown," the children said to each other.

"Can we make a crown, Mrs. Wilkins?" Christie asked.

"I think so," Mrs. Wilkins replied. "After I read the story, we'll try to make a crown."

Margie sat down, and Mrs. Wilkins began to read. On other days the children always chatted about the story. Today, as soon as the story was finished, the children only wanted to talk about the crown.

"It must be a gold crown," said Margie.

"I'll see if I have some gold cardboard," said Mrs. Wilkins, pulling open a closet door. She looked through one of the shelves, and soon the children saw her pull out a piece of gold cardboard.

"It must have points all around the top," said Bruce. "Crowns always have points around the top."

Mrs. Wilkins laid the sheet of cardboard on a table. Then she said, "I'll have to measure Debbie's head, so it will be the right size." Mrs.

Wilkins looked around for Debbie. "Where is she?" she asked.

"She went to get a drink of water," Christie replied.

Bruce was standing next to her, so Mrs. Wilkins said, "Come, Bruce, I'll measure your head." With a tape measure, she measured Bruce's head. Then she marked off the inches on the cardboard with a ruler.

"Can I make the points?" Philip asked. Philip was very proud of being the best artist in the class.

"You can make the points," Mrs. Wilkins replied.

After Philip had drawn the edge of the crown, Mrs. Wilkins let Christie cut it out with the scissors. Then she fastened the back of the crown with paper clips. "Now, Bruce," she said, "try on the crown." Mrs. Wilkins placed the crown on Bruce's head. It fit nicely.

By this time Debbie was back. "May I try it

on?" she asked, "since I'm going to be the first one to wear it."

Bruce took it off and put it on Debbie's head. It went down over Debbie's ears and sat like a collar around her neck, for Debbie was a very little girl. Everyone laughed.

"That will never do!" said Mrs. Wilkins. "We shall have to fit the crown for each wearer with paper clips." When Mrs. Wilkins had changed the position of the paper clips, Debbie could wear the crown.

"Debbie will be the first birthday princess," said Christie.

"Next month I'll be a birthday king," said Philip.

"And we'll have to move the paper clips again," said Chuckie.

The following Thursday Christie met Mrs. Wilkins at the school-yard gate. Mrs. Wilkins was carrying a parcel. "We're going to bake the

birthday cake today, aren't we?" Christie asked.

"I have a box of cake mix in this parcel," Mrs. Wilkins replied. "And three eggs."

"What about the pink candles?" Christie asked.

"I have a box in my desk," Mrs. Wilkins answered.

In the afternoon, when Mrs. Wilkins asked Bruce to plug in the oven, all the children were excited about baking their first birthday cake.

Christie brought out the clean mixing bowl.

Sara opened the box of cake mix.

Mark measured a half cup of water.

Philip asked if he could break the eggs. He broke one into the bowl and the other on the floor. "Oops! Sorry about that!" he said. "If my cat were here, he'd eat it. My cat loves eggs. We need a cat, Mrs. Wilkins. Don't you think we need a cat?"

"We need another rabbit!" said Margie. "We need a papa rabbit. Then we would have baby rabbits."

"I think we need a cat," said Philip.

"We do not need a cat," said Mrs. Wilkins. "We just need someone who can break eggs into the bowl."

"Let me do it! I can do it!" came from every child.

"Mark, you do it!" said Mrs. Wilkins. "I only brought three eggs. If you drop the one that is left, we can't make the cake."

Mark held his breath as he picked up the egg. "Oh, be careful," said Christie.

"Don't crack it hard!" said Margie.

The rest of the children were holding their breath.

"Stop bugging me!" said Mark, as he cracked the egg against the edge of the bowl.

"Oh, the eggshell went in!" Philip cried out. "The eggshell's in!"

As Mark fished the eggshell out of the bowl, he said, "Well, I got the *egg* into the bowl."

Then Mrs. Wilkins beat the batter while the

children watched. As she poured it into the shiny cake pan, the children murmured, "Yummy! Yummy!"

After the cake was placed in the oven, the children watched the clock. They spent most of the next hour running to look through the glass window in the door of the oven. At last the cake was done, but it had to cool before the pink icing could be smoothed over it.

Mrs. Wilkins put the make-believe cake on the top shelf of the closet. "Now that we have a real birthday cake we don't need the make-believe one," she said, as she locked the closet door.

By the time the children left at the end of the day, the cake had been frosted. The beautiful pink birthday cake with seven pink candles was left standing on the same plate where the make-believe cake had always stood. It was covered with the same glass cover. The gold crown was resting on top of the glass cover. Everything was ready for Debbie's birthday the next morning.

The following morning Debbie was surrounded by her friends. They met Mrs. Wilkins at the front door and followed her to their room. As they entered the room, Christie called out, "Now Debbie must put on her crown."

"Yes, indeed!" said Mrs. Wilkins. "Come, put on your birthday crown." Mrs. Wilkins led Debbie to the table where she had left the cake and the crown. The table was empty. "Why, where are they?" Mrs. Wilkins exclaimed. She looked all around the room. "Where can they be?" she asked.

The children were speechless. Mrs. Wilkins dashed out of the room. As each child came into the room, he was told, "The birthday cake's gone, and the crown is gone, too."

When Mrs. Wilkins returned, the children saw that her hands were empty. She said to the children, "No one on this floor knows anything about our birthday cake or the crown. The office doesn't know anything about them either."

The children's faces looked very sad, and Debbie was close to tears.

"I'm sure we'll find that everything is quite safe," said Mrs. Wilkins, trying to bring some cheer to the children. "We must go to the assembly now. We don't want to be late for the third grade's play."

Mrs. Wilkins's children marched into the assembly hall. Not a single face was smiling. They sat down and looked at the drawn curtains on the stage. They joined in the opening song, but the voices of the first grade were very weak. No one felt like singing.

When the song ended, a boy from the third grade stepped out from between the curtains and said, "This play that we are about to present is called *The King's Birthday*."

The first grade pricked up their ears and sat up.

The curtains opened, and there sat a boy in a long royal robe, wearing the gold crown that Debbie should have been wearing. In front of him, on a table, was the birthday cake that Mrs. Wilkins and her first grade had made the day before. The children pointed to the cake and whispered to each other, "That's our cake! That's our cake!"

Christie didn't listen to a word that the children on the stage were speaking. She just thought about Debbie's crown and the birthday cake. The play went on and on. Christie thought it would never end.

At last the children heard the king say, "And now I shall cut my birthday cake."

The whole first grade stood up and cried out, "Don't cut it!"

Debbie shouted as loud as she could, "That's my birthday cake and that's my crown!"

The children on the stage were so surprised that they didn't know what to do. Children all over the room stood up to see what was the matter with the first grade. Debbie's big sister called out, "That's my little sister's birthday cake!"

Everyone was glad when the curtain closed on the king and his subjects and the birthday cake.

When the first grade returned to their room, Mrs. Garvey, who taught the third grade, was standing by the door. She was holding the birthday cake and the crown. "I'm sorry!" she said. "I sent one of the boys to borrow the make-believe cake that you have always loaned us. We didn't know that it was a real cake until the children called out to us."

Debbie and all of the children were happy again. Debbie wore her gold crown, and the children sang, "Happy birthday, dear Debbie, happy birthday to *you.*" When they ate the birthday cake, they knew it was real. They all agreed that it was yummy!

Chapter 5

AND FOR CAREFUL CAT

CHRISTIE'S FIRST GRADE had been working with clay. "Really, truly clay," Christie told her mother. "What we make can be put in a hot oven, and when it's done, it's as hard as this cup," said Christie, picking up her cup of cocoa.

"We don't use our cook oven, 'cause it doesn't get hot enough," Christie explained. Mrs. Wilkins is going to bake everything we make in a hot, hot oven that she has at home. It's called a kiln."

"What have you made?" her mother asked.

"I made a bird," Christie replied. "Most of the children made plates and saucers, but I made a bird. Mark made a giraffe, and Debbie made a pig. Bruce made a horse, and Philip made a cat. He says it looks just like his cat Charlie."

When Mrs. Wilkins brought the children's clay pieces back, she placed them on a shelf that was fastened to the wall, not far from the rabbit's cage. The children stood by and admired their work.

Philip pointed to his cat and said, "That cat looks just like my Charlie Cat." Then he said to Mrs. Wilkins, "I wish I could bring Charlie Cat to school, so he could live here. Charlie Cat misses me when I'm in school all day. He's a nice cat. You would like him. Charlie Cat's a very good cat."

"We need another rabbit," said Christie, "A nice rabbit! Cupcake will never have babies if we don't get another rabbit."

"I have a cat," said Philip. "I don't have a rabbit."

After a while more children began asking if they couldn't have a cat. Finally one day, when Philip again asked if he could bring his cat, Mrs. Wilkins said to him, "Is this cat house-broken?"

"Oh, yes!" Philip answered. "Charlie Cat's very good. He uses the litter pan!" Then, with his eyes shining, he said, "Are you going to let me bring him?"

Mrs. Wilkins looked at all the children and said, "How many of you would like to have a cat?"

Every hand went up except Chuckie's. "Who wants a cat?" he said.

"I know why you don't want a cat," said Philip, " 'cause you can't eat cat food."

"That's right!" Christie agreed. "He ate Cupcake's cornflakes, but he doesn't like to eat cat food."

Chuckie just grinned.

"Please, Mrs. Wilkins, can't we have the cat?" said Christie. "It would be nice to have a cat."

"Very well, Philip," said Mrs. Wilkins. "You can bring the cat."

"Oh, that's good!" said Philip. "You'll like Charlie Cat."

"Why do you call him Charlie Cat?" Chuckie asked.

"Everybody has a last name," Philip replied. "Charlie's last name is Cat."

"That's silly!" said Chuckie. "I don't call my dog Brownie Dog."

"Course not!" said Philip. " 'Cause he's not a cat. If Brownie was a cat, you'd call him Brownie Cat."

"Brownie couldn't ever be a cat," said Chuckie, " 'cause Brownie's a dog. That's what he is! He's a dog. And I'm glad he's a dog, because cats are always up to something. I'll bet your cat's always up to something. I don't like cats."

Philip put his hands on his hips, and with his feet spread apart he looked at Chuckie. "Charlie Cat is a very nice quiet cat."

"I'll bet he flies all over the place, jumping on things and knocking things over," said Chuckie. "I know cats!"

"Charlie Cat is a very careful cat," said Philip. "Very careful."

The following morning Philip arrived with his cat. He carried him proudly. He walked around the room, showing him to each child, saying, "Here's Charlie Cat."

"Oh, he's a funny-looking cat," said Chuckie. "I never saw a cat with blue eyes before."

"I guess you never saw a Siamese cat before," said Philip. "Charlie Cat's a Siamese cat."

"I don't like Siamese cats," said Chuckie. "I wouldn't have one if you gave it to me. I knew one once. He was terrible."

When Philip showed the cat to Mrs. Wilkins, she patted Charlie Cat and said, "He's very beautiful."

Philip was pleased to have Mrs. Wilkins praise his cat, but he dropped Charlie Cat when she asked, "Where is the litter pan?"

"Oh," he said, "my mother put it in the car. I'll see if she's still outside." Philip took off as fast as he could go.

As soon as Charlie Cat dropped to the floor, he sprang up like a rubber ball. Then he seemed to fly through the air and landed right on top of the rabbit's cage.

"Oh," cried Christie, "he's after my rabbit!" Christie ran to the cage. "Scat!" she cried.

Charlie Cat let out a meow like nothing that

Christie had ever heard before. It was more like a yowl than a meow. Christie backed away from the cage. All of the children watched the cat as he looked down at the rabbit. When they saw him poke his paw down through one of the holes in the wire that covered the top of the cage, Christie cried out, "He's trying to reach Cupcake with his paw!"

"Scat! Scat!" Christie kept crying, but Charlie Cat did not scat. Instead he poked his other paw through another hole in the wire.

"Mrs. Wilkins!" Christie called out. "He's got both paws down inside the cage!"

Mrs. Wilkins came to see what was alarming the children. When she saw Charlie Cat lying on top of the cage with both paws hanging down inside, she laughed. He waved his paws back and forth, but he couldn't reach the rabbit. When the children saw that Mrs. Wilkins was laughing, they laughed too.

Just then Philip came back with the litter pan

and a can of cat food. "I caught my mother," he said. "Where's Charlie Cat?"

"Your terrible cat is after my rabbit," said Christie.

"Oh, Charlie Cat wouldn't harm a flea," said Philip. "He's just very playful and friendly." Then he said to Mrs. Wilkins, "Where shall I put the litter pan?"

"Put it in the corner of the room," Mrs. Wilkins replied.

Philip placed the litter pan in the corner of the room and went back to the rabbit cage. He patted Charlie Cat.

"That cat looks wild to me," said Chuckie. "You sure he isn't a wildcat?"

"Course not," said Philip. "He's a very friendly cat."

"I hope he's a quiet cat," said Mrs. Wilkins, who was beginning to think she had made a mistake when she had said that Charlie Cat could come to school.

"Oh, he's very quiet," said Philip.

At that moment Charlie Cat pulled his paws out of the rabbit's cage and leaped to Mrs. Wilkins's desk. "I hope you don't mind if Charlie Cat takes a nap on your desk, Mrs. Wilkins," said Philip. But Charlie Cat had no intention of taking a nap. Instead he leaped from the desk to the shelf where the pottery pieces that the children had made stood.

The children looked up from their books that they had just started to read. "Oh," cried Debbie, "that cat's going to knock our things off the shelf."

"No, Charlie Cat is very careful. He walks all around, but he never does any damage. Wait until you see how careful he is."

Before long the children were able to see how careful Charlie Cat was. First he knocked down Mark's giraffe. Then Debbie's pig crashed on the floor. Next came Bruce's horse and Christie's bird. Philip ran to the shelf just as his pottery cat fell down.

Philip picked up Charlie Cat, and the children picked up their broken animals.

"I thought you said that cat was a careful cat," said Christie.

Philip looked troubled. "I don't know what's the matter with him. Charlie Cat's such a good cat."

"He's crazy!" said Chuckie. "He's a crazy cat."

"You're just saying that because he isn't yours," said Philip.

"I wouldn't have a cat like that," said Chuckie. "A crazy old cat!"

"I think he feels a little bit strange," said Philip. "He'll be all right when he gets used to school."

"He's strange all right," said Bruce. "He's no pussycat. He's a wildcat."

Philip put Charlie Cat down, and he sniffed his way to the litter pan. In a few minutes Charlie Cat began making yowls. "That means Charlie Cat's hungry," said Philip.

"Then feed him," said Mrs. Wilkins. "Feed him so that he will stop making that terrible noise."

Philip opened the can of cat food, and Charlie Cat settled down to eat his lunch. "He'll go to sleep after he eats his lunch," said Philip, when he came back to join the reading group. "He always takes a nap after he eats."

"I hope he takes a long nap," said Mrs. Wilkins.

Charlie Cat didn't take long to eat his food.

When he finished, he washed his face with his paws and quietly padded across the room to the sofa. There was nothing on the sofa but Mrs. Wilkins's red sweater. Charlie Cat jumped up on the sofa and settled down on top of Mrs. Wilkins's sweater.

As soon as the children finished their reading lesson, Christie and Debbie and Mark set to work gluing their broken animals together again. After a while Bruce joined them. He looked at the pieces of pottery lying on the table. He picked them up and examined each one closely. Then he said, "A leg of my horse is missing. Anybody see a leg of my horse? I only have three legs for my horse."

No one paid any attention to Bruce's question. "I say," he asked, "did anybody see the leg of my horse? How can I fix my horse if I have only three legs?"

The children were too busy putting their animals together to look for the horse's leg.

Debbie was the first to finish. She placed her pig on the shelf and said, "Tomorrow I'll paint my pig pink, and the cracks won't show hardly at all."

Christie was mending her bird's wing. "Christie," said Bruce, "have you got my horse's leg?"

"Course not!" Christie answered. "Birds don't have horse's legs."

"Well, my horse had four legs," said Bruce, "and I can only find three. Phil, have you got my horse's leg?"

"What would a cat do with a horse's leg?" Philip replied.

By this time Mark had finished putting his giraffe together. He placed it on the shelf and said, "It looks pretty good. Anyway it has a nice long neck."

Bruce looked at the giraffe on the shelf and said, "Mark, that giraffe has the longest neck I ever saw on a giraffe." Bruce reached up to touch it.

"Don't touch it!" said Mark. "I just got it together. All giraffes have long necks."

Bruce looked hard at the giraffe. Then he said, "Well, they don't have horse's legs in their necks, and your giraffe has my horse's leg in his neck."

"He has not got your horse's leg in his neck," said Mark.

"I'll show you," said Bruce. "You take it down, and I'll show you."

Mark lifted his giraffe down from the shelf, and Bruce pointed to the part that he was sure was his horse's leg. "There!" he said. "That's my horse's leg, and you better take it out before the glue dries and my horse's leg is in your giraffe's neck forever."

"If I take that piece out, my giraffe's neck won't be long enough," said Mark. "He won't look like a giraffe at all. *Something* goes in there."

Christie went to the wastebasket to throw a piece of paper away. As she did so she saw a piece of clay in the basket. She picked it up and said, "Look, Mark! Is this your giraffe's neck? I guess this piece flew into the basket."

"That's it," said Bruce. "Now hurry up and give me my horse's leg."

Mark was able to take the giraffe's neck apart, and before long Bruce's horse was standing on four legs again. Then Mark glued his pieces together once more. Now the giraffe had a long enough neck to be a giraffe.

Soon it was time for lunch. When the bell rang, Charlie Cat woke up and jumped off the sofa. Mrs. Wilkins went to the sofa and picked up her sweater. When she put it on, she saw that there was a large hole in the sleeve. "Now how did that happen!" she exclaimed. "There was no hole in my sweater this morning."

"Oh, Mrs. Wilkins!" said Philip, looking scared. "I'm afraid Charlie Cat made that hole. You see Charlie Cat likes to eat wool. I'm very sorry he ate your sweater."

"Why does he eat wool?" Mrs. Wilkins asked. "Isn't the cat food enough for him? Just look at my sweater!" Mrs. Wilkins held it up so the children could see what Charlie Cat had done.

"I told you he's a bad cat," said Chuckie. "He's a real wildcat."

"He ate his lunch, and then he ate Mrs. Wilkins's sweater," said Debbie.

"I guess he ate it for his dessert," said Chuckie.

"Chuckie, that isn't funny," said Mrs. Wilkins. "How would you feel if he ate your sweater?"

"I'd send him home," said Chuckie.

"That is exactly what I am going to do at the end of this day," said Mrs. Wilkins. "Now we must go to lunch."

An hour later, when Mrs. Wilkins and the children returned to their room, pieces of torn paper lay all over the floor, all over the tables, and all over Mrs. Wilkins's desk. Charlie Cat had been busy tearing up papers for a whole hour. He had torn up the children's paintings and drawings, their work papers, their spelling papers, and the stories that they had written.

Mrs. Wilkins and the children stood staring at the mess that Charlie Cat had made. "Now look what this cat has done!" said Mrs. Wilkins.

"Oh," said Philip, "it's because we forgot to give him a paper bag. He just loves a paper bag. He gets inside and just loves it. I guess Charlie Cat was looking for a paper bag."

"I'll be glad when this day is over," said Mrs. Wilkins, "but now let's pick up all these pieces of paper. And Philip, please hold your cat for the rest of the afternoon. Then take him home with you."

The children set to work picking up the papers. They were all mad at Charlie Cat for tearing up their paintings.

Philip held Charlie Cat until the time came to go home. When he said good-bye, he said to

Mrs. Wilkins, "I'm sorry Charlie Cat didn't behave very well, and I'm sorry he ate that hole in your sweater. He's really a very careful cat."

Mrs. Wilkins patted Charlie Cat and said, "Perhaps he doesn't like going to school."

"I guess that's it," said Philip, as he left the room.

Eric, a new little boy in the class, said to Mrs. Wilkins, "I've got a horse, and I wondered whether you would like—"

Before he could finish what he was saying, Mrs. Wilkins said, "No, Eric! No! I do not want a horse."

"If you could see this horse," Eric continued.

"No, Eric," said Mrs. Wilkins. "I don't want the best horse in the world."

"It's a beautiful horse," said Eric.

"I'm sure it's a beautiful horse," said Mrs. Wilkins.

"It sure is," said Eric. "It came off a merry-go-round."

"Oh!" said Mrs. Wilkins. "Well, I'll think about it."

The following morning Philip arrived with a box under his arm. He handed it to Mrs. Wilkins and said, "I've brought you something. It's from Charlie Cat and me."

Mrs. Wilkins took the box and said, "Thank you, Philip."

"Open it! Open it!" said Philip. "See if you like it!"

Mrs. Wilkins opened the box and folded back some tissue paper. Then she held up a new red sweater. "What a beautiful sweater!" she said. "Thank you very much, Philip."

"You're welcome," said Philip. "I'm sorry I can't give back all those papers that Charlie Cat tore up. I should have remembered to bring a paper bag."

Chapter 6

AND FOR CHRISTMAS COOKIES

COLD WEATHER had arrived early and with it came snow and ice. The children came into school in warm snowsuits with their hoods over their heads. The ones who had forgotten their mittens had icy fingers, and Mrs. Wilkins had to rub them in order to get them warm again. All the children were glad to get into their cozy schoolroom.

One morning in December, when the children were sitting on the floor in front of Mrs. Wilkins, she told them about the cookie contest. Mrs. Wilkins said, "This month the school will have Cookie Day instead of Cupcake Day, and the best cookies will receive a prize."

Bruce looked up and said, "What's the prize?"

"It will be a blue ribbon," Mrs. Wilkins answered.

"That's a funny prize," said Chuckie. "A blue ribbon! You can't eat a blue ribbon."

The children laughed at Chuckie.

"It isn't a funny prize," said Margie. "They give blue ribbons at dog shows. I know because my grandfather raises dogs, and his dog won a blue ribbon once."

"Horses get them, too," said Philip. "I've got an uncle who has a horse, and—"

Mrs. Wilkins spoke up and said, "Excuse me, Philip. We should like to hear about your uncle's horse at another time. Just now we're talking about cookies."

"Will our mothers make the cookies instead of cupcakes?" Christie asked.

"Yes, the mothers will make cookies," Mrs. Wilkins replied, "but I have a different idea for you children, and I think you will like it."

Christie looked at Mrs. Wilkins's face, and she knew that Mrs. Wilkins was pleased with the idea, for her eyes were beginning to twinkle. "Tell us!" said Christie.

"Can you keep a secret?" Mrs. Wilkins asked the children.

"Yes, yes," they answered.

"Very well!" said Mrs. Wilkins. "We are the only class in the school that has an oven."

"I know! I know!" Christie called out. "*We'll* bake cookies!"

"And we'll win the prize!" said Philip.

"When is Cookie Day?" Margie asked.

"It is next Friday," Mrs. Wilkins answered. "We shall have to bake the cookies on Thursday."

Christie counted on her fingers. Today was Monday, then Tuesday, Wednesday, and Thursday. She could hardly wait to bake the cookies.

"Christmas is coming," said Debbie. "Will they be Christmas cookies? Will we put red and green sugar on them?"

"Oh, yes!" the children cried. "Red and green sugar."

Mrs. Wilkins laughed. "If you want to make Christmas cookies with red and green sugar, you may," she said.

"If the cookies have holes in the center, we could tie red and green ribbons on them," said Margie.

"Then people could take them home to tie on their Christmas trees," said Debbie.

"Who's going to give the prize?" Mark asked.

"Somebody will have to taste a lot of cookies before he says which cookies are the best," said Chuckie. "Can I be the taster?"

"I'm afraid not," Mrs. Wilkins answered. "The judge will be the lady who cooks on T.V. Perhaps you have seen her." Some of the children nodded their heads.

On Thursday morning Mrs. Wilkins arrived at school with long rolls of cookie dough wrapped in wax paper. She had mixed up the dough the night before.

"Did you bring the red and green sugar?" Christie asked.

"Yes, indeed!" Mrs. Wilkins replied. "And five cookie cutters with holes in the center."

Before school started, Mrs. Wilkins spread sheets of wax paper on the tables. As soon as the bell rang, the cookie baking began. Mrs. Wilkins divided the children into five groups. There were four children in each group. "Each group will have a captain," said Mrs. Wilkins. "Christie will be captain of the first group, Mark for the second, Sara for the third, Bruce for the fourth, and Philip for the fifth."

"What does the captain do?" Mark asked.

"The captain will cut off dough for the cookies with a knife," Mrs. Wilkins explained. "Then one helper will make the cookie with a cookie cutter. Another will sprinkle the sugar."

At this point the children's voices rose in a chorus. "I want to sprinkle the sugar!"

"Everyone can't sprinkle the sugar," said Mrs. Wilkins. "Each captain must select a sugar sprinkler."

The children turned to their captains. "Can I? Can I? Can I?" could be heard all over the room.

Mrs. Wilkins raised her voice above the clatter. "The fourth child in the group will place the cookies on the cookie pan and put the pan in the oven."

"Who takes them out of the oven?" asked Philip.

"I will take them out of the oven," Mrs. Wilkins replied. "Be sure your hands are clean," she added, handing a roll of cookie dough to each captain.

Now the children scurried around. Everyone wanted to wash his hands at once, but finally the children got busy at the tables. Each group had three small dishes, one with red sugar, one with green sugar, and one with flour. "Don't forget to dip your cookie cutter into the flour so that the dough won't stick to the cutter," Mrs. Wilkins warned.

Soon there was sugar trouble. "Robbie's upset the green sugar all over the floor! What shall we do, Mrs. Wilkins?" asked Sara.

"Just make red cookies," Mrs. Wilkins replied. "Robbie, sweep up the sugar."

"Chuckie's eating the sugar!" Bruce cried out.

"I'm not eating it out of the dish. I'm just eating it when it falls off the cookie," said Chuckie. "I like the green sugar. The green sugar is best."

"Well, you're messing up the table with your fingers," said Bruce.

"Chuckie, stop eating the sugar," Mrs. Wilkins called to him.

Before long Christie said, "Mrs. Wilkins, our cookies are ready for the oven."

Mrs. Wilkins opened the oven door, and Margie put the pan into the oven. Soon the odor of baking cookies filled the room.

Suddenly there was trouble in Bruce's group. Chuckie stuck out his tongue, and Bruce said, "Oh, something awful is the matter with you. Your tongue is bright green! You're gonna be sick."

"Oh, look at Chuckie's tongue!" said Becky. "It's green as grass! You're going to be awful sick."

Chuckie's eyes grew round. He walked away from his group to the sofa. He lay down.

"Mrs. Wilkins!" Bruce called out. "Chuckie's sick."

Mrs. Wilkins went to the sofa. She looked down at Chuckie and said, "What is the matter, Chuckie?"

"I'm sick!" he replied. "My tongue's turned green, and it hurts awful. I think I'm going to throw up."

Mrs. Wilkins took hold of Chuckie's arm and lifted him up. "There's nothing the matter with you, Chuckie," she said. "It's just the green sugar that has made your tongue green. If it hurts, you must have bitten it."

Chuckie stuck out his green tongue and felt it gently with his finger. "I guess it's all right now," he said. "But it did hurt."

"Mrs. Wilkins, Mrs. Wilkins! The cookies are burning!" This cry came from the cookie watchers.

Mrs. Wilkins rushed to the oven while

Chuckie rejoined his group. She opened the oven door and pulled out the pan of cookies. They were a bit too brown, but the children were glad to see that they were not burned.

Soon the other pans were ready for the oven. One after another they went in and were taken out. When all were baked, the children counted them. They had made sixty cookies. The children thought that they were the best cookies they had ever seen.

After the tables were cleaned, the wax paper thrown away, and the dishes as well as the children's hands washed, each child ate a cookie. They nodded their heads and agreed that they were the best cookies they had ever eaten.

"Those cookies will get the blue ribbon for sure!" said Chuckie, licking sugar off his fingers.

"Just wait until they get red and green ribbons tied on them," said Christie. "Everybody will want to buy our cookies."

The next morning, when the children came

into their room, the cookies with their red and green ribbons were laid out on a large tray. The children thought they were beautiful. Christie was allowed to carry the tray into the lunchroom, and the rest of the children followed her. She placed the tray on a long table where other cookies were laid out. Each plate or tray of cookies had a white envelope on top of the cookies piled on it. The children knew that inside of each envelope was the name of the person who had made the cookies. Inside the envelope on their tray was a piece of paper that said, "Made by Mrs. Wilkins's first grade."

All during the morning the children kept saying to Mrs. Wilkins, "Do you think we'll get the blue ribbon?"

Mrs. Wilkins would answer, "We just have to wait and see."

At a quarter to twelve the bell rang for the first and second grades to go to lunch. Now they would see who had won the blue ribbon.

As soon as the bell rang, Mrs. Wilkins's children rushed out the door. They didn't have far to go, for the lunchroom was right across the hall. They reached the room before the children from the other classes arrived. Quickly they ran to the big table where all the cookies were and looked for the blue ribbon. There it was, bright blue with a shiny gold star. To the delight of all Mrs. Wilkins's first-grade children, it was resting on their tray of cookies.

"We won!" they shouted together. "We won the blue ribbon!" Some of the children jumped up and down they were so excited. Then before anyone could say, "Tom Thumb!" the children in Mrs. Wilkins's class bought up all the cookies they themselves had made.

"I'm going to hang mine on my Christmas tree," said Christie.

"I'm not!" said Chuckie, with crumbs all over his chin. "I say, don't put off until tomorrow, what you can eat today!"

Chapter 7

AND FOR CANDY CANES

AS THE CHRISTMAS holidays grew near, everyone could see that it would be a white Christmas. The snowfall had been heavy, and many children could be seen sledding on the hills after school.

Some of the hills were too steep for the little

children, and Mrs. Wilkins warned her first graders not to sled on them.

"That's what my mother tells me," said Christie. "Steep hills are for big children."

"I like the steep hills," said Robbie. "You go faster! It's fun when you go fast. I'm not afraid of the steep hills. The little ones are for sissies!"

"I hope no one is listening to Robbie," said Mrs. Wilkins. "The steep hills are dangerous for little children. I hope you will all keep away from them, and I mean Robbie, too."

One morning, just a week before school closed for the holidays, Robbie was absent from school. "I wonder where Robbie is this morning," said Mrs. Wilkins.

"I saw him yesterday," said Mark. "He had his sled with him. I guess he was going over to that big hill where my mother won't let me go. My mother never lets me do anything."

Later in the morning Mrs. Wilkins and the children heard the news. Robbie had broken his leg, sledding, and he was in the hospital. The children were shocked.

"Oh!" said Mark. "I'm glad I didn't go sledding on that hill after all. I guess my mother's right!"

"It's terrible about Robbie," said Christie. "I guess he'll be in the hospital at Christmas."

"He should have listened to you, Mrs. Wilkins," said Chuckie, "but now we have to do something to make his Christmas happy."

"We can send him some flowers," said Margie.

"Flowers!" said Chuckie, scornfully. "He should have something nicer than flowers when his leg's broken. We should send him a Christmas tree."

"A whole Christmas tree?" exclaimed Christie. "How could we send Robbie a whole Christmas tree?"

"Well, we could send him things to hang on his Christmas tree, couldn't we, Mrs. Wilkins?" Chuckie asked.

"That is very thoughtful, Chuckie," said Mrs. Wilkins. "We could begin by making strings of popcorn."

"That's good!" said Chuckie. "We better start popping the corn, 'cause it will take a long time to make those strings."

"You'll have to take turns at the popper," said Mrs. Wilkins. "Some of you can start right now. Chuckie, Christie, Eric, Rebecca, and Bruce can be the first to make popcorn today. The rest of the children can stay here with me."

The five children got up, and Mrs. Wilkins said, "There's a jar of popping corn in the closet." The children were delighted. Popping corn was fun! They liked to watch the little hard kernels open into snow-white balls.

As the corn popped, the white fluffy balls were poured from the popper into a large wooden bowl on a table. The children sat around the table and dipped into the bowl. They picked up the pieces for their string. Soon they were all busy with needle and thread, stringing the popcorn.

Chuckie, as he worked, picked up a piece for his string and then a piece for his mouth. Several times he went to the water fountain.

After some time Christie said, "Stop eating the popcorn, Chuckie. You eat it the way you ate Cupcake's cornflakes."

"I love popcorn!" said Chuckie, eating another piece. "Trouble is, it makes me awful thirsty. I have to get another drink of water."

Chuckie didn't make much progress with his string. He was either eating the popcorn or going to get a drink of water. By the time all of the corn from the jar had been popped, the children had long strings of popcorn. Chuckie's, however, was very short.

When the long strings were shown to Mrs. Wilkins, Chuckie left his by the popper and went to the sofa. There he lay down.

"Mrs. Wilkins," Philip called out, "Chuckie's on the sofa again!"

Mrs. Wilkins left her group of children and came to the sofa. She looked down at Chuckie, whose face was screwed up into a knot. "What's the matter, Chuckie?" she said.

"I feel as though there's a football inside my tummy," said Chuckie.

"He ate the popcorn," said Christie, "and then he drank a lot of water."

The children gathered around and looked at Chuckie. "It's all that popcorn," said Bruce.

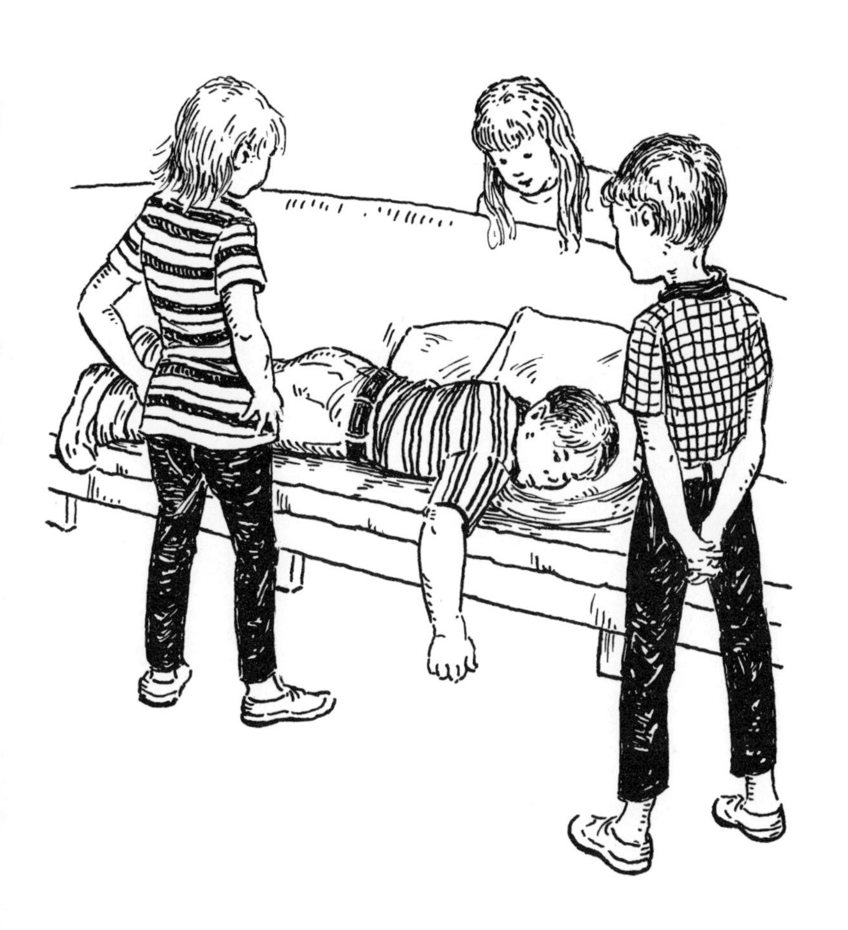

"Yepper!" the children said to each other, shaking their heads. "He's full of popcorn."

"Just like that time with the cornflakes," said Mark. "That time the cornflakes were inside his shirt, remember?" The children nodded their heads. "This time it's inside *him,*" Mark finished.

Chuckie groaned. Mrs. Wilkins leaned over him and whispered to him. "Do you remember when we were studying about farms?" Chuckie nodded his head. Mrs. Wilkins continued. "Which of the animals ate the most corn?"

Chuckie murmured, "The pigs."

"That's right," said Mrs. Wilkins, "but you're a little boy. You just lie still, and you'll feel better soon."

When school was over for the day, Chuckie was able to get up and go home on the bus.

The next morning, when sharing time came, the children were gathered around Mrs. Wilkins. Some were sitting on the floor, and some on little chairs. Christie was the first to raise her hand. "Christie has something to share with us," said Mrs. Wilkins.

Christie got up and stood beside her teacher. "I brought this angel to go on Robbie's Christmas tree," she said, holding the angel in front of her. The children thought it was beautiful, for it was made of gold paper and white net. "I know why angels go on Christmas trees," said Christie.

"Tell us, Christie," said Mrs. Wilkins.

"Because the angels' song is 'Glory to God in the highest, and on earth peace, good will toward men.' "

Then Mark's hand was raised, and Mrs. Wilkins called him to her side. Mark held up a large gold star. "I brought this star for Robbie's tree," he said, "and I can tell you why stars go on the top of Christmas trees. It's the star of Bethlehem that the shepherds saw in the sky on Christmas Eve. It led them to the baby Jesus."

Sara's hand went up. When Mrs. Wilkins asked her to come to her, Sara held up a tiny brass candlestand. It had eight branches. "This is a menorah," she said. "In my home we have a holiday that comes at the same time of year called Hanukkah. It celebrates the triumph of the Jews over their enemies through their faith in God. We have a big menorah, just like this little one. It has eight candles, and we light one candle each day for eight days. When they are all lighted, it is beautiful."

Sara looked up at her teacher and said, "I had some candles to put in this little menorah, but I lost them on the way to school."

"Never mind," said Mrs. Wilkins. "We can put birthday candles in your menorah." Mrs. Wilkins went to her desk and found some birth-day-cake candles. After Sara had placed the candles in the menorah, Mrs. Wilkins put it on the shelf with the children's pottery pieces.

Several of the children had pictures to show and tell about. Some had brought little toys, and Margie had a tiny pair of wooden shoes with her.

She stood up to tell about the shoes and said, "When my mother was a little girl, she lived in Holland, and at Christmas time they didn't hang up their stockings. They left their wooden shoes out for Santa Claus to fill."

"You wouldn't get as much in a shoe as you do in your stocking," said Philip. The children all agreed with Philip. They were glad that they would hang up their stockings on Christmas Eve.

"I'm going to be sure to put my shoes away in the closet, where Santa Claus won't see them," said Chuckie. "Then he won't think I left my shoes out for him to fill."

The children laughed at Chuckie.

"You know what!" said Chuckie. "We should have candy canes for Robbie's Christmas tree. You can't have a Christmas tree without candy canes. Where can we get some?"

"I wonder why they put candy canes on Christmas trees?" said Christie.

" 'Cause they're pretty," said Margie.

"There is another reason," said Mrs. Wilkins,

"and I'll tell you about it." The children looked pleased, for they loved to hear stories.

Mrs. Wilkins began. "You know that wonderful, jolly man you call Santa Claus?" The children nodded their heads. "Well, in many countries, far away across the ocean, they call him Saint Nicholas. Now in pictures of Saint Nicholas we see him carrying a staff." Mrs. Wilkins looked around at the children and said, "Can anyone tell us what a staff is?"

"It's like a cane," said Bruce.

"The ones shepherds carry have a crook on the end," said Becky.

"That's right," Mrs. Wilkins agreed. "So, many years ago, someone thought it would be nice to make the staff of candy, and they called it a candy cane."

"Because of Saint Nicholas!" Christie and Bruce called out.

"Maybe because of the shepherds that saw the star," said Margie.

Debbie spoke up. "My grandmother lived in

Germany when she was a little girl. She told me about Saint Nicholas last night before I went to bed. She calls him Nikolaus. My grandmother lived in the mountains where there was a lot of snow. In the winter it snowed every night. Two weeks before Christmas, Nikolaus would come out on the streets to see the children and talk to them. But you know what? He didn't carry a cane; he carried a broom."

"Why did he carry a broom?" one of the children asked.

"Maybe to sweep the snow," said Mark. "He couldn't carry a staff and a broom, could he?"

Debbie went on with her story. "My grandmother said that all the children would run after Nikolaus, and if anybody was naughty he would give them a good whack with his broom."

The whole first grade laughed very hard. "I'm glad Santa Claus doesn't do that," said Christie. "We just go to see him in a big store and sit on his lap."

"We have to get some candy canes for Robbie's tree," said Chuckie once again. "Where are we going to get the candy canes?"

"I don't know," said Mrs. Wilkins. "I tried to buy some this morning, but the candy store was sold out."

Now that the children had heard about candy canes they all felt that Robbie must have some for his Christmas tree.

The very morning of the last day before the holidays began, Eric came into the room with a box. His face was shining, and when he handed the box to Mrs. Wilkins, he chuckled and said, "Here's something for Robbie's Christmas tree."

"Why, Eric," said Mrs. Wilkins, "you look as happy as old Santa himself. What have you brought us?"

"You'll see!" Eric replied.

The children gathered around Mrs. Wilkins. "What is it? What is it?" they asked, as they looked at the box. When Mrs. Wilkins lifted the lid, they all shouted, "Candy canes! Candy canes!"

Eric looked very pleased when Mrs. Wilkins said, "How wonderful! You've brought us just what we needed. And you've brought so many!"

"My father works in a candy factory. I told him we needed candy canes for Robbie's Christmas tree, so here they are."

"There are too many for the tree," said Chuckie. "Guess we can each have one, can't we, Mrs. Wilkins?"

Mrs. Wilkins laughed. "You'll have to ask Eric," she said.

"Sure!" said Eric, as he handed Chuckie a candy cane. "Merry Christmas!"

"Thanks!" said Chuckie. "Merry Christmas to you."

At the end of the day, the children left with boxes in their hands. They were the things to go on Robbie's Christmas tree. Christie also had her rabbit. She was taking Cupcake home for the holidays.

"What's in your box, Chuckie?" asked Mark.

"My popcorn string for Robbie's tree!" Chuckie replied.

"Your popcorn string!" said Mark. "It isn't big enough to go around my neck."

"Never mind," said Chuckie. "I have a Christmas tree for Robbie, and my dad's going to take me to the hospital this afternoon. He says you can all come along."

By four o'clock there was a crowd of children around Chuckie's house. They all had boxes of trimmings for Robbie's tree. Soon they were packed into Chuckie's father's station wagon. The car moved slowly on the icy street, but soon they were on their way. They were taking the Christmas tree to Robbie. As Chuckie said, "When you have a broken leg, you *need* a Christmas tree!"

Chapter 8

AND FOR CINNAMON BUN

ONE DAY Chuckie got on the school bus with a basket. It was the kind of basket that is made for carrying cats. Chuckie sat down beside Christie. "What's in that basket?" Christie asked.

"You'll be surprised!" Chuckie replied.

"Well, what is it?" said Christie.

"It's *my* rabbit!" Chuckie answered. "My Uncle Jim gave it to me for my birthday."

Christie was surprised. "A really, truly rabbit?" she exclaimed. "I want to see it. Let me see it."

"I can't open the basket here on the bus," Chuckie answered. "He might jump out."

Christie looked very pleased. "That's nice," she said. "Now Cupcake will have company. I think Cupcake will like that."

"No!" said Chuckie. "My rabbit isn't going to live in the cage with Cupcake. My rabbit's very special. He's going to live in the whole room."

All the children on the bus were interested in Chuckie's rabbit. "You can't let a rabbit loose in the room," said Bruce, who was sitting across from Chuckie. "He'll be jumping all around!"

"What color is he?" Christie asked.

"He's brown," replied Chuckie. "He's a very special rabbit."

"What's special about a brown rabbit?" Tommy asked from the seat behind Chuckie.

"He comes from Belgium," Chuckie answered. "That's what makes him special."

"We have brown rabbits hopping all over our backyard," said Tommy.

"Not like Cinnamon Bun," said Chuckie. "Cinnamon Bun is special."

"Cinnamon Bun!" exclaimed Christie. "Is that his name?"

"Yepper!" Chuckie answered.

Christie called out to the children in the bus, "Chuckie's rabbit's name is Cinnamon Bun!" Then to Chuckie she said, "Can't I look in the basket and see Cinnamon Bun? I'll just peep!"

"Well, okay," said Chuckie, "but real quick."

Chuckie lifted the lid of the basket just as the bus went over a big bump in the road. It bounced the basket right off Chuckie's lap. As it fell to the floor, the rabbit jumped out. "There goes the rabbit!" the children cried out.

The rabbit ran toward the front of the bus just as the bus reached a bus stop. A large group of children were standing outside, waiting for the door of the bus to open.

"Don't open the door! Don't open the door!" Chuckie called out to Mr. Clark, the bus driver.

Mr. Clark turned around in his seat and said, "What's the matter?"

"It's my Cinnamon Bun!" Chuckie called back.

"Why don't you hold onto your cinnamon buns?" said Mr. Clark. "What have your cinnamon buns got to do with my opening the door?"

"It's not cinnamon buns!" said Chuckie. "It's Cinnamon Bun! My rabbit! He got out of his basket, and he's loose in the bus. If you open the door, he'll jump out."

Meanwhile, the children outside were knocking on the door of the bus. They wanted to come in.

Mr. Clark rolled down the window and called to them. "Can't open the door," he shouted. "Got a loose rabbit in here."

All the children inside the bus were trying to catch the rabbit, but the rabbit moved very fast. He ran up and down under the seats. Soon shouts of "I've got him! I've got him!" rang out. They were followed by "Oh, dear! He got away!"

Mr. Clark joined the hunt while the children outside kept calling, "Can't we come in now?"

"Not until we catch the rabbit," Mr. Clark called back from under a seat.

The children inside the bus were on their hands and knees. Cinnamon Bun had disappeared.

"He's hiding someplace," said Chuckie.

"Chuckie!" said Mr. Clark. "This is the second time you have given me rabbit trouble. I think you should keep away from rabbits."

Bang! Bang! Bang! The children outside were knocking on the door. "Can't we come in and hunt the rabbit?"

"We're not playing a game, Hunt the Rabbit!" Mr. Clark called back. "You'll have to wait until we find it."

"We'll be late for school," someone cried from outside.

"Can't be helped!" Mr. Clark answered.

Suddenly Chuckie called out, "I found him! Here he is! He was hiding under my sweater that I dropped on the floor." Chuckie held up Cin-

namon Bun by the loose skin on the back of his neck. "Look, Mr. Clark! Isn't he a beautiful rabbit? Did you ever see a rabbit as beautiful as my Cinnamon Bun?"

"He's okay!" said Mr. Clark, who didn't care for any rabbits at that moment. "Stick him in the basket, and keep him there. I don't want to see any more rabbits on this bus."

At last Mr. Clark opened the door, and the children from outside rushed in. "Where's the rabbit! I want to see the rabbit! Who's got the rabbit!" they shouted.

"Don't open that basket!" Mr. Clark called out to Chuckie.

The new children that had just boarded the bus were disappointed, but they settled themselves in the seats and the bus rolled on. Chuckie was delighted to tell them about his rabbit. "His name is Cinnamon Bun!" he said. "He's a very special kind of rabbit."

"Oh, I'm so glad he's a *he!*" said Debbie, who

had just arrived. "Now we'll have baby rabbits."

"Silly!" said Chuckie. "Everybody knows that *he* rabbits don't have babies."

"I know that!" said Debbie. "I'm not stupid! But Cupcake will have the babies."

"No, no!" Chuckie cried out. "Cinnamon Bun is not going to live with Cupcake! Cinnamon Bun is going to live outside the cage, but he'll look in the cage sometimes. He'll go up and look in the cage at Cupcake, and he'll say, 'Poor Cupcake! Poor Cupcake! Has to live in a cage! Has to live in a cage!' "

"We take her out and pet her," said Christie.

"But you have to put her back again," said Chuckie.

When the bus reached the school, Mr. Clark opened the door and said, "Now you're not late but hurry along."

As Chuckie got out with his basket, Mr. Clark said, "I hope I don't have any more rabbit trouble with you."

Debbie was right behind Chuckie, and she said to Mr. Clark, "Maybe there will be baby rabbits soon."

"Well, don't bring them into my bus," said Mr. Clark. "I don't want my bus turned into a rabbit hutch."

"There won't be any babies," Chuckie called back.

"That's what you think!" said Debbie.

As each child entered the room, each one said to Mrs. Wilkins, "Chuckie's brought a rabbit."

When Chuckie brought the basket to Mrs. Wilkins, she already knew that there was a rabbit inside. She watched while Chuckie lifted the beautiful rabbit out of the basket. He held it up and said, "This is my very own rabbit. His name is Cinnamon Bun, and nobody can touch him but me."

"Then you will have to take Cinnamon Bun home and keep him there," said Mrs. Wilkins. "In this room we share everything."

"Well, I won't put him in the cage with Cupcake," said Chuckie, " 'cause he's a very special rabbit."

"We can't have him hopping around the room," said Mrs. Wilkins, "so if you won't put him in the cage with Cupcake, you will have to keep him in the basket."

"Can I take him out and love him when I want to?" Chuckie asked.

"Yes, you can," Mrs. Wilkins replied.

All the children wanted to see Cinnamon Bun. They wanted to pet him the way they petted Cupcake, but Chuckie kept the rabbit in his arms and close to his chest.

Christie took Cupcake out of the cage and brought her to Chuckie. "See, Chuckie!" said Christie. "I think Cupcake would like to make friends with Cinnamon Bun."

Chuckie held his rabbit away and said, "She might bite Cinnamon Bun."

"Cupcake doesn't bite," said Christie.

"She might kick Cinnamon Bun," said Chuckie. "The way she kicked me."

"She didn't mean to do it. Everybody knows Cupcake is very friendly," said Christie.

Chuckie thought for a minute. Then he held Cinnamon Bun so that the two rabbits' heads were near each other. The children laughed when the rabbits poked their noses together.

"See!" said Christie. "They like each other. They could live together in the cage."

"No!" said Chuckie, and he put Cinnamon Bun back in the basket.

When lunchtime came, Mrs. Wilkins said to Chuckie, "Don't you think it would be better to put Cinnamon Bun in the cage with Cupcake?"

"He's okay!" said Chuckie. "He's fine."

The children and Mrs. Wilkins left the classroom to go to the lunchroom. Mrs. Wilkins closed the door behind her. When they were halfway down the hall, Chuckie said, "I better go back and see if I fastened the lid of the basket."

"Very well," said Mrs. Wilkins. "Be sure it is fastened."

Chuckie returned to the room. He tested the fastening on the basket. It was all right, but when he left the room he forgot to close the door.

After the children had eaten lunch they went out into the school yard to play. Mrs. Wilkins went with them.

An hour later they formed a line and came back into the school building. As they walked through the hall toward their room, they could hear a dog barking. The sound grew louder as they neared the door of their room. Mrs. Wilkins began to run ahead of the children. Soon Chuckie and Christie caught up with Mrs. Wilkins. They could hear scuffling and thumping noises and sharp barks. They knew that a dog must be in the room.

Mrs. Wilkins and Chuckie rushed into the room, but Christie was afraid and held back. From where she stood she could see that a large black dog had the handle of Cinnamon Bun's basket between his teeth. He was beating it on the floor and growling at it.

Mrs. Wilkins ran to the dog and grabbed hold of the handle of the basket. "Give that to me!" she said.

The dog snapped at Mrs. Wilkins, but she held on to the basket and wrenched it out of the dog's mouth. The dog turned and ran out of the room.

"Oh, Mrs. Wilkins!" Chuckie cried. "Is my rabbit all right?"

Mrs. Wilkins opened the basket and picked up the rabbit. He was trembling with fright. She held him in her arms. "Poor little thing!" she said. The children gathered around Mrs. Wilkins.

"Is he all right?" Chuckie asked again, pressing against Mrs. Wilkins.

"He's all right, but he's scared," Mrs. Wilkins answered.

"You were brave, Mrs. Wilkins," said Chuckie. "Wasn't Mrs. Wilkins brave?" he called to the children.

"Oh, yes! She was very brave," they shouted.

"That dog must have wandered into the school," she said. "He must have smelled the rabbits."

"He was trying to open the basket, wasn't he?" said Bruce.

"We came just in time," Mrs. Wilkins said. "In a few more minutes he would have had the basket open."

"Would he have killed Cinnamon Bun?" Chuckie asked.

"I'm afraid so," said Mrs. Wilkins.

Chuckie held his rabbit tight. Later in the day, he said to Mrs. Wilkins, "Maybe I better put Cinnamon Bun in the cage with Cupcake. It's safer there."

"That is a very good idea, Chuckie," said Mrs. Wilkins.

Chuckie carried Cinnamon Bun to the cage and put him inside. Cinnamon Bun began to nibble on the lettuce leaf that Cupcake was eating. Cupcake moved over and made room for Cinnamon Bun.

"Oh, now we'll have baby rabbits, won't we, Mrs. Wilkins?" said Debbie.

"Perhaps so," Mrs. Wilkins replied. "It would be nice, wouldn't it?"

The children agreed that having baby rabbits would be very nice.

"They'll be little Cupcakes," said Christie.

"No, they won't!" said Chuckie. "The children always have their father's name. They'll be little Cinnamon Buns."

"They'll be Cinnamon Bunnies! That's what they'll be," said Debbie. "Cinnamon Bunnies!"

The children laughed. Soon Chuckie and Christie and all the children were looking forward to the arrival of the Cinnamon Bunnies.

Now that Chuckie had a rabbit of his own, he

loved it very much. He carried it home over the weekends in the kitty basket, and he was very careful to keep the lid on so that Cinnamon Bun wouldn't get free in the bus. Chuckie always scurried past the bus driver when he had his rabbit with him. He didn't want any more rabbit trouble on the bus. Chuckie knew how the bus driver felt about rabbits in his bus. He didn't like them! Not *one little bit*!

Chapter 9

AND FOR COOKING FOR DADDY

CUPCAKE and Cinnamon Bun were soon living happily in the cage together. The children expected baby rabbits almost at once. When Mrs. Wilkins told them that babies could not be born for at least twenty-eight to thirty days, the children thought that was a long time to wait.

At last the day came when Christie discovered that Cupcake was pulling her fur out. "Oh, Mrs. Wilkins!" Christie cried. "Cupcake is tearing her fur out with her teeth."

Mrs. Wilkins and all the children in the room came to look at Cupcake. "Sure 'nough!" said Chuckie. "She's getting ready to have babies! My Cinnamon Bun is going to be a father!"

Straw had been placed in the cage so that Cupcake could make a nest for the babies. Now she would line the nest with her fur. Another cage had been built for Cinnamon Bun, because he would have to live by himself while the little ones were with the mother. When the children asked why, Mrs. Wilkins told them that Cinnamon Bun might step on the babies and kill them. The children agreed that to have the babies killed would be a terrible thing.

"We better take Cinnamon Bun out right away," said Chuckie, "and put him in the other cage."

"Do it now, Chuckie," said Mrs. Wilkins.

Chuckie lifted his rabbit out of the cage and put him in the other one. Then Cupcake was alone, busily pulling out her fur and making the nest.

"I hope the babies come before school closes for the summer," said Margie.

"They will be born long before then," said Mrs. Wilkins.

While the children waited for this important event, they became better readers. They learned how to spell more words and to add, subtract, multiply, and divide numbers. They borrowed books from the school library and read them.

The library was on the third floor. The children liked to climb the stairs to the library. One day, when the children went to the library, Christie's mother was there helping the librarian. So was Mark's mother and Sara's. The children were pleased to see their mothers.

When the children returned to their classroom, Christie said, "It's nice to have our mothers come to school, isn't it, Mrs. Wilkins?"

"It is, indeed," Mrs. Wilkins agreed.

"Our fathers never come," said Philip. "Only our mothers."

"I wish our daddies could come," said Christie.

"Perhaps they are waiting to be invited," said Mrs. Wilkins.

"Well, let's invite them," said Bruce.

"When somebody invites you, they invite you to a party," said Christie. "You have to be invited to something."

"My daddy couldn't come to a party," said Debbie. "My daddy has to go to work."

"What about a breakfast party?" Mrs. Wilkins suggested. "Perhaps they could come to breakfast on their way to work."

The children's eyes sparkled. "That's a great idea!" Mark exclaimed.

"We could cook the breakfast in our oven," said Christie.

"We have to make coffee," said Philip, " 'cause my father drinks coffee with his breakfast. He drinks three cups."

"And orange juice," said Margie.

"And scrambled eggs," Sara added.

"Don't forget the toast," said Chuckie. "My father eats a lot of toast."

"My father can't come," said Becky. "My father has to be at work at nine o'clock."

"If we invite your fathers to breakfast, you will all have to come to school earlier. You will have to be here at eight o'clock," said Mrs. Wilkins.

The children called out, "I can come at eight o'clock. I can come."

"Very well!" said Mrs. Wilkins. "How many of you want to invite your fathers to breakfast?" Every hand went up.

That very day the children wrote their invitations, asking their fathers to breakfast the following Thursday.

"We don't have a toaster or a coffeepot," said Philip at the end of the day. "How will my father have his three cups of coffee if we don't have a coffeepot?"

"Don't worry, Philip," said Mrs. Wilkins. "I'll bring my toaster and a coffeepot."

"I just hope the babies don't come until Friday," said Mrs. Wilkins. The children wondered why.

Before the end of the day, Mrs. Wilkins told the children exactly what they were to do on Thursday morning. They were to be divided into four groups. One group would make the toast, one would scramble eggs, one would pour the orange juice, and one would wait on the tables.

"What about my father's coffee?" Philip called out.

"I'll make the coffee," said Mrs. Wilkins.

On Thursday morning ten of the children arrived with their fathers. The other fathers were unable to come, because they had to get to work early. Christie and her father were the first to arrive.

"Daddy," said Christie, "come and see the nice nest Cupcake is making for her baby rabbits."

Christie led her father to the cage. She looked down at the nest. To her great surprise, the nest was filled with a tight mass of baby rabbits. "Oh," cried Christie, "the babies are here!"

Then she put her finger on her lips and said, "They're asleep. We mustn't make any noise."

Mrs. Wilkins almost dropped the coffeepot. "Not today!" she cried. "What a day to have baby rabbits arrive!" When she looked into the cage, she said, "What a lot of rabbits! How many do you suppose there are?"

"Nine or ten, I should think," said Christie's father.

As the children came into the room, they gathered around the cage. "Let me see! Let me see!" was heard again and again. "Oh, can I have one? Can I?"

Christie kept saying, "Sh-sh!"

They don't look like rabbits," said Philip. "They look like little mice. They don't have any fur on them."

"Course not!" said Mark. "They won't get fur until their eyes open."

When Chuckie arrived, he was so excited about the little rabbits that he went out to the front steps of the school and shouted the news to the big children in the school yard. "We got Cinnamon Bunnies! My rabbit Cinnamon Bun is a father! Come and see our Cinnamon Bunnies!"

This announcement brought more children into the first-grade room. They all wanted to see the Cinnamon Bunnies. Christie went around with her finger on her lips saying, "Sh-sh! They're asleep!" More and more children came, and soon the room was filled with children wanting to see the baby rabbits. The fathers were forgotten.

"Why don't you have a contest to name one of them. Then whoever wins the contest gets the rabbit," said Jack Carpenter, Chuckie's brother from the third grade.

"Oh, let's!" said Christie. "Mrs. Wilkins, can we have a contest to name one of the babies?"

"Yes, yes!" Mrs. Wilkins replied. "But now you have to make breakfast for your fathers. Just leave the rabbits alone."

The children couldn't leave the rabbits alone. The egg scramblers kept running to the cage to see if any more babies had been born. The toast makers kept going to pick out the rabbit each one wanted, although they all looked alike. The orange juicers kept walking to the cage with glasses of orange juice in their hands. None of the table waiters would leave the cage. They were afraid more bunnies would be born and they wouldn't be there to see them.

Suddenly someone cried out, "She's nursing them now! She's nursing the babies!" Every child in the room stopped what he was doing. There was a rush to the cage.

"I'm sure there will be no more babies," said Mrs. Wilkins, handing cups of coffee to the fathers. The children didn't believe her. They felt that if there were eight or ten, there could be more.

Christie kept going around saying, "Sh-sh-sh!" But no one paid any attention to Christie.

Finally the fathers took over. They scrambled their eggs, they made their toast, and they poured their orange juice.

When the children saw that breakfast was ready, they finally left Cupcake and the rabbits. They sat down at the tables to eat what their fathers had prepared. Mark looked up at his father. With a fork full of scrambled eggs, he said, "This is a good idea, isn't it, making breakfast for our fathers?"

Before his father could reply, Christie said, "Oh, yes!" She crunched up a bite of toast, and then she said to her father, "Aren't you glad, Daddy, that we invited you to breakfast?"

"I never had such an exciting breakfast before," her father replied.

"There's just one thing," said Christie. "This should have been Cupcake Day. The bunnies should have been born on Cupcake Day. Then we could have had cupcakes to eat."

"I wonder how many will be white like Cupcake and how many will be brown like Cinnamon Bun," said Bruce.

"Maybe some will be brown and white. Maybe white with brown spots," said Debbie.

"Or brown with white spots," said Chuckie.

"They don't have any fur at all now," said Eric. "I wonder how soon they'll get fur."

"When their eyes open, they will begin to get fur," said Christie.

Philip called to Mrs. Wilkins, "How soon will Cupcake have more babies, Mrs. Wilkins?"

"Oh, my!" Mrs. Wilkins exclaimed. "I hope she won't have any more very soon."

Margie looked up at her father and said, "It

was nice, wasn't it, Daddy, that you could come to breakfast the very day the bunnies were born?"

"Wouldn't have missed it!" her father replied.

"Daddy," said Christie, "we'll have to have another cage for all these bunnies."

"That's right!" said Chuckie. "Maybe our fathers could make us a cage this morning."

"There's a lot of good wood out back of the school," said Philip.

The fathers got up from the tables. "I think we had better go to work," said Christie's father.

Before the fathers could reach the door, the door opened and Jack from the third grade came in. He said to Mrs. Wilkins, "Our class has brought some names for the baby rabbits. Course, whoever wins won't take the rabbit today."

"Course not!" said Christie. "They haven't got their eyes open yet."

"We just wanted to get our names in," said Jack, as he left.

"Read the names, Mrs. Wilkins! Read the names!" said many of the children.

"Say good-bye to your fathers first," said Mrs. Wilkins.

"Good-bye, Daddy!" they called, waving their hands. "Good-bye!"

"Good-bye!" the fathers replied. "Thank you for a very nice breakfast."

"Come again!" the children called back.

Then Mrs. Wilkins opened the pieces of paper on her lap. She began to read the names written on them. Some of the names were Jumpie and Pinkie and Buttercup and Daisy. There were girls' names and boys' names. At last Mrs. Wilkins read aloud, "Sticky."

"That's it! That's it!" Chuckie called out. "Sticky Cinnamon Bunny!"

All the children laughed. "That's it!" they said.

Chuckie and Christie were sent to the third grade to announce the result of the contest. When the little girl who had written *Sticky* on her slip of paper heard that she had won a rabbit, she was delighted.

"You can pick it out just as soon as the baby rabbits get their fur," said Christie.

Just before lunch period, a delivery boy came into the first-grade room. He was carrying a cardboard box. "Is this Mrs. Wilkins's first grade?" he asked.

"Yes, it is," Mrs. Wilkins replied. The boy handed the box to Mrs. Wilkins and left the room.

Mrs. Wilkins looked at the box. There was a note fastened on the top of it. She opened the note and read it. Then she laughed. She held it up and showed it to the children. "Here's a present for all of you," she said. Then she read the note to the children.

It said, "Thank you for the good breakfast. Here's something for your lunch. Happy birthday to the bunnies."

The children crowded around Mrs. Wilkins to see what was in the box. When she lifted the lid, the children saw that the box was full of cupcakes.

"Cupcakes!" Chuckie exclaimed. "I wonder why they didn't send cinnamon buns."

Chapter 10

BUT NOT FOR PEANUT BUTTER

THE BABY RABBITS grew larger every day. As soon as their eyes were open, they became very lively. There were nine altogether. Some were white and some were brown and some were spotted. The largest of the brown ones was given the name Sticky, and Sandra who had won the contest was looking forward to taking it home as soon as it was old enough to leave the mother.

The first-grade children called the little rabbits by different names almost every day. "That one is Spunky!" Chuckie would say.

"No, it isn't!" Debbie would reply. "That other one's Spunky. I ought to know because I picked that one out. It's going to be mine."

Every child in the class wanted a rabbit to take home, but Mrs. Wilkins said they must ask their parents if they could have one. "Oh, I can have one! I can have one!" they all said.

"You must bring me a note from your mother first," said Mrs. Wilkins.

Mrs. Wilkins waited to hear. A whole week went by, and no one brought a note saying that a child could have a rabbit. The children just kept talking about having a rabbit.

"I always wanted a white rabbit," said Debbie, "but my mother says you can't have a rabbit when you live in an apartment. I guess she's right."

"I can't have one," said Bruce, "because my mother says she doesn't like things that jump."

"My mother says I can't have one," said Sara, "because she says if you have one rabbit, pretty soon there are more rabbits, and she isn't going to have rabbits all over the house."

The children shook their heads sadly, and one after the other murmured, "No rabbits!"

Meanwhile, the baby rabbits grew until Cupcake's cage was so full that Cupcake was pushed into the corner most of the time. There was one less when Sandra came for the rabbit she had won in the contest. She took Sticky into her arms and said, "Sticky is going to live in our third-grade room, because my mother doesn't like rabbits as much as I do. She says their hairs get up her nose and make her sneeze. We have a cage for Sticky in our classroom, and everybody is glad Sticky will live with us." Sandra left the room carrying the rabbit.

"Maybe we could give a rabbit to each room

in the school," Christie suggested. Notes were sent to all the classes in the school, asking if they would like to have a rabbit. No one wanted a rabbit.

A week before school was to close for the long vacation, Chuckie came into the room with a face like a thundercloud. "Whatever is the matter with you, Chuckie?" Mrs. Wilkins asked.

"I got trouble!" Chuckie replied. "I can't take Cinnamon Bun home!"

"What do you mean, you can't take him home?" Mrs. Wilkins asked.

"My mother says we're going away for the whole summer," said Chuckie, "and there's nobody to take care of my rabbit."

"Oh, that *is* bad news!" said Mrs. Wilkins. "Now we have another rabbit to find a home for."

"My Cinnamon Bun is such a special rabbit," said Chuckie, with tears in his eyes.

"I know he's a very special rabbit," said Mrs. Wilkins. "We'll have to think of something."

"I wouldn't give him to just anybody," said Chuckie. "I would only give him to somebody very special. Somebody who deserved a very special rabbit. Do you think the President of the United States would like to have a very special rabbit? Cinnamon Bun came all the way from Belgium. I'd take him down to Washington in his cat basket and give him to the President. I'd give him the cat basket too. It's a very special basket. The President could use the basket when he goes on picnics to carry his peanut-butter sandwiches in."

"That basket is full of rabbit hairs," said Margie. "The rabbit hairs would get all over the President's peanut-butter sandwiches."

"How do you know he likes peanut-butter sandwiches?" Philip asked.

"Everybody likes peanut-butter sandwiches!" Chuckie exclaimed. "Everybody!"

Mrs. Wilkins interrupted the conversation. "Whether the President likes peanut-butter sandwiches or not," she said, "I don't think the President wants a rabbit, not even a special one."

"Can't we write to the President and ask him if he can tell us who would like to have a very special rabbit?" Chuckie asked.

"Chuckie, we can't write to the President of the United States," said Mrs. Wilkins.

"We did write to him," said Chuckie. "Don't you remember? We wrote about pollution."

"That's different," Mrs. Wilkins replied. "The President is interested in pollution. He is not interested in rabbits."

Chuckie looked up at Mrs. Wilkins. There were wrinkles across his forehead. "I didn't like rabbits at first," said Chuckie, "but when you have one, you love your rabbit. The President would love Cinnamon Bun if he had him for his own rabbit."

"We are not going to write to the President, Chuckie," said Mrs. Wilkins. "He has enough problems."

After two more days went by, the time had come to find some place for the rabbits. School would soon close. Chuckie seemed especially worried about Cinnamon Bun.

"Today," said Mrs. Wilkins, "I'll telephone to the zoo and ask them if they will take our rabbits."

"Can't you telephone to the zoo right now?" Chuckie asked.

"Very well!" Mrs. Wilkins replied. There was a telephone in the room, so Mrs. Wilkins looked up the telephone number of the zoo in the telephone book and dialed it.

The children gathered around their teacher, and Chuckie pressed against her. "I want to hear what the man says," he said. "If you don't put the receiver too close to your ear, I can hear what he says."

They didn't have to wait long for the zoo to answer the telephone. "Hello, this is the zoo!" Chuckie heard.

"It's them!" he said to the rest of the class. "It's the zoo!"

Mrs. Wilkins spoke into the telephone. "This is the first-grade class," she said, "and we have some rabbits. We should like to give them to the zoo."

"Oh, we have loads of rabbits," was the reply.

Chuckie scowled. "Tell him about mine," he said. "Tell him Cinnamon Bun is very special."

Before Mrs. Wilkins could say anything, the voice on the other end added, "Now if you had a Belgian rabbit, we would be interested. Our Belgian rabbit just died, and we're looking for another one."

"We have a Belgian rabbit," said Mrs. Wilkins. "He's the father of the eight little ones."

"Well then, bring them along!" said the man at the zoo. Chuckie's face was covered with smiles.

"We'll bring them day after tomorrow," said Mrs. Wilkins. When she had hung up the receiver, she saw that the children were happy.

"I thought we might have to put those rabbits out in the ash can," said Eric. "I'm glad the zoo wants them."

"Will we all go to the zoo with the rabbits?" Christie asked.

"I think that would be nice," Mrs. Wilkins replied. "We can take a picnic lunch and eat it at the zoo."

All the children cried out, "Will we have peanut-butter sandwiches?"

Mrs. Wilkins laughed. "Yes, if that is what you want."

"Sure, sure!" they replied. "Peanut-butter sandwiches!"

Before the end of the day, Mrs. Wilkins had arranged for a bus to take them to the zoo. She had also asked Christie's mother and Bruce's mother to go with them. The two mothers offered to bring the peanut-butter sandwiches.

When the day arrived for the trip to the zoo,

it was warm with bright sunshine. It was a perfect day for a picnic.

All the peanut-butter sandwiches were packed in a picnic basket. "Is there milk?" Margie asked. "I have to have milk with peanut-butter sandwiches."

"We can get milk at the zoo," Mrs. Wilkins replied. "There's a counter where they sell milk."

"I don't want to eat my peanut-butter sandwiches at a counter," said Bruce. "I want to sit on the grass. It isn't a picnic unless you can sit on the grass."

"You can sit on the grass," said Mrs. Wilkins. "Anyone who wants to eat his sandwiches sitting on the grass can do so. Now let's get these rabbits into the bus."

"Cinnamon Bun isn't going in the cage," said Chuckie. "I'll take him in the cat basket, 'cause he's too special to go with those other rabbits."

After the cage with the rabbits was placed in the bus, the children got in. Mrs. Wilkins and the two mothers came aboard, and the picnic basket was placed in the back of the bus. The only rabbit left behind was Cupcake. Christie would take Cupcake home for the summer vacation.

The children were excited when they reached the zoo. Some of them had never been to the zoo before. As they stepped out of the bus they could hear the lions roaring.

The man who worked at the zoo and had charge of the rabbits was waiting for the bus to arrive. He had a small cart on wheels to receive the cage. He looked over the eight rabbits and said, "Where's the Belgian?"

"He's in this basket," said Chuckie. "Can I see where he's going to live, and can I come and visit him?"

"Sure!" the man replied. "Anytime."

The bus driver called to Mrs. Wilkins and said, "I'll be back for you at one thirty. I'll meet you right here." The bus drove away.

The children followed the man with the cage. When he opened it and the rabbits ran out, the children laughed. "They'll be happy here," said the man.

Chuckie didn't look very happy when he handed Cinnamon Bun to the man. As he smoothed the rabbit's fur, he said, "You sure I can come and see Cinnamon Bun?"

"Anytime!" said the man, as he examined the rabbit. Then he said, "He's a beautiful rabbit! Very special! We'll put him in a special place."

Chuckie beamed with pleasure. He looked up at Mrs. Wilkins and said, "Didn't I say so? Didn't I, Mrs. Wilkins?"

"You certainly did!" Mrs. Wilkins replied.

The children finally left the rabbits and went off in a line, two by two, to visit the rest of the zoo. As twelve o'clock drew near, the children began to say, "I'm hungry! When do we have the picnic? When do we eat our peanut-butter sandwiches?"

Mrs. Wilkins looked at the two mothers and said, "Where did we leave the picnic basket?"

"Oh," cried Christie's mother, "we left it in the bus! How dreadful!"

The children looked at each other and said, "The peanut-butter sandwiches are in the bus!" Their faces were very sad.

"We can't have a picnic without our sandwiches!" Chuckie cried. "I just love peanut-butter sandwiches," he moaned.

"We shall have to see whether we can get sandwiches at the milk counter," said Mrs. Wilkins. "I'll lead the way."

"Maybe they have peanut-butter sandwiches," said Mark.

When they reached the counter, Mrs. Wilkins asked if they sold sandwiches.

"Yes!" replied the man behind the counter.

"Peanut butter?" the children called out.

"No." the man replied. "I just have cheese today."

"Cheese!" the children groaned. "Just cheese!" Some of the children wouldn't eat the cheese sandwiches. Some ate part of a sandwich and left the rest on their plates. But Chuckie ate his own and what remained of Mark's.

Mark looked at Chuckie and said, "You know what, Chuckie?"

"What?" Chuckie replied.

"Everybody is going to call you Fatso pretty soon!" said Mark. Chuckie just grinned.

When the children had drunk their milk and eaten as much as they wished of the sandwiches, they walked to the place where the bus would pick them up. When it arrived, they climbed in. Then there were shouts of, "There's the picnic basket!"

"Now we can eat our peanut-butter sandwiches!" Chuckie cried.

Mrs. Wilkins and the mothers opened the basket and handed the sandwiches to the children. As the bus bounced along they ate them. The children came back to school, dragging their feet. They were tired, but they were not hungry, for they were full of peanut-butter sandwiches. They all agreed that it had been a wonderful day.

"I guess Cupcake's been very lonely," said Christie, "and I guess she's hungry." Christie went to Cupcake's cage and gave her a stick of carrot.

"I'm going to take her home today," said Christie to Mrs. Wilkins. "But I'll bring her back when school opens in September. Then maybe she'll have some more babies."

"Yes, yes!" the children called out.

"Then we can go to the zoo again," said Mark, "and take the bunnies."

"That's right!" said Chuckie. "Only we mustn't forget the peanut-butter sandwiches."

"Oh, Mrs. Wilkins!" Christie exclaimed. "I just remembered! We won't be in the first grade anymore. We'll be in the second grade."

"That's right," Mrs. Wilkins replied. "I'll

miss you. You'll be second-grade children, and the bunnies will be second-grade bunnies."

"First grade has been fun," said Christie, "and I guess second grade will be fun too. Especially if we have the bunnies."